Countdown to Christmas Eve!

Dianna Houx

Reading Order

1.) Countdown to Christmas
2.) Countdown to Valentine's Day
3.) Countdown to Easter
4.) Countdown to Mother's Day
5.) Countdown to 4th of July!
6.) Countdown to Halloween!
7.) Countdown to Thanksgiving!
8.) Countdown to Christmas Eve!
9.) Countdown to New Beginnings
10.) Countdown to a Wedding

I recommend reading the books in order. There is an overarching storyline that starts in book 1 and continues throughout the series. Plus, it's more fun that way!

Contents

-Twenty-

G race tossed the phone down on the couch in frustration as tears stung the back of her eyes. Despite all her careful, if not frenzied, planning for her upcoming wedding, everything that could have gone wrong did. Things were utterly and completely hopeless. She walked over to the sliding glass door and stared out at the fields visible from the farmhouse as she tried to reign in her emotions.

"What's wrong?" Cole asked as he looked up from the saddle he was working on. "More bad news?"

"That was Pastor Allen calling to inform me he's had a family emergency and will be out of town for the next few weeks. He gave a list of pastors who could stand in for him, but..." Grace's voice trailed off.

Cole stood and walked over to her, pulling her into his arms. "But you don't want a stranger marrying us, do you?" he asked gently. He kissed the top of her head as he swayed side to side in an effort to soothe her.

A muffled sound came from his chest as she did her best to stifle a sob. "How is it possible for everything to go so wrong?"

"I know it feels personal, but it's not," he assured her. "We are rushing things a bit. Would it really be so bad if we gave this a little more time and got married next month instead?"

Grace lifted her head to look at him, her mouth open and her eyes wide in horror. "But I don't want to wait to become your wife. Christmas is the most magical time of the year—at least it was," she said sadly, lowering her head to hide her tears.

"Hey," he said, lifting her chin with his finger. "Christmas is still magical, okay? And we can still have a Christmas-themed wedding in January." He shook his head. "Baby, we've spent our entire relationship running around like chickens without heads. It would be nice to take the time to do this right—and, you know, maybe even enjoy the process instead of being so stressed out all the time."

"I guess you're right," she admitted reluctantly. "Our wedding has kind of felt like an afterthought since we've been trying to squeeze it in alongside our latest Traditional Christmas Experience."

Cole nodded in agreement. "Exactly. And if we wait till next month, we should be able to go on a honeymoon right after the wedding instead of having to wait. Wouldn't that be nice?"

She could tell he was trying his hardest to sell her on this new plan, despite the fact they had little choice in the matter. Not only had Pastor Allen backed out, but the church was closed for repairs after the recent storm, and all the other venues were already booked due to the holiday season. As if that weren't enough, Bea was unavailable to make the cake, Jilly was dealing with a family crisis, they couldn't find a photographer, and the list went on—and on. It would appear trying to plan a last-minute wedding in December was a bad idea.

"Yes, it would be nice," Grace relented. "I guess it's official, then: the wedding is off until we can pick a new date in January."

Rebekah walked into the room and set her purse down on the table with a thud. "I must be imagining things, because I'm pretty sure I just heard you say the wedding is off. There is no way those words actually came out of your mouth," she said to Grace.

Tears stung Grace's eyes again, so she took a deep breath in a vain attempt to hold them back. "You heard correctly," she said sadly.

"The wedding is not off—it's just postponed," Cole explained to a visibly shocked Rebekah.

She nodded as a look of understanding washed over her face. "I know this is hard, but think of all the things we can do now that we have more time."

"Like what?" Grace asked petulantly. She knew her friend was only trying to help, but she would gladly elope with Cole and leave all this stress to the bridezillas of the world. Not that she was claiming all brides were bridezillas, just that having a large wedding had never been her dream. Grace had never been the type to like being the center of attention. She hadn't been planning her dream wedding since she was young, nor did she have a clear vision she wanted to bring to life. All she wanted was to marry the man she loved with all her heart and spend the rest of her life with him.

"Well—for starters—now that we have more time, I'll be able to order a hundred doves for you to release as soon as you say 'I do.'" Rebekah held up one finger. "There's time to find your princess dress, complete with a matching tiara." She raised a second finger. "We'll be able to get the ice sculpture." She raised a third finger and opened her mouth to list the next impossible idea—but burst out laughing instead. "The look on your face!" she said, holding her stomach as she laughed. "I wish I had recorded this!"

"I really hope that means you were joking," Grace deadpanned.

Rebekah took a deep breath and wiped her eyes. "Of course I am, silly. I was just trying to cheer you up. Seriously, though, this doesn't have to be a bad thing. It will be nice to give your wedding the attention it deserves."

"That's what Cole said," Grace admitted. "I'm not happy about it, but I guess I will accept it."

Cole hugged her again before letting go and returning to his task. "This will also give you more time to focus on turning the B&B into a winter wonderland. I missed out on that last year—and I'm excited to experience it. Maybe you could even bring a little Christmas cheer out to the farm!"

"Decorating is one of your favorite things to do," Rebekah sang while nudging Grace with her elbow.

Grace laughed. "Fine, you win. Want to help me?"

"I thought you'd never ask," Rebekah replied. "When I was young, my mother would hire decorators to decorate our house. It looked like something out of a magazine, but I always felt it lacked true Christmas spirit. We were never allowed to touch anything or help in any way. In fact, one time, I made an ornament in art class to hang on the tree, but later found it in the trash. My mother said it clashed with the aesthetic."

Rebekah tried to laugh it off, but Grace could tell she was still hurt by the memory. It was hard to believe any mother could be so cruel—but this was the same woman who had cut off her daughter for refusing to marry the man of her mother's choice, so...

"I'm sorry you went through that," Grace said softly. "But you'll have plenty of opportunities to create new memories with us. And I, for one, would be honored to display your homemade ornaments front and center on my tree!"

A smile lit up Rebekah's face as she hugged Grace. "Thanks. You really are the best!"

"Let's see if you still feel that way once you see the mountain of decorations we need to bring down from the attic!" Grace's smile faded when she remembered how much damage the storm had done to her precious heirlooms after a tree fell on the roof. She, Granny, and Cole had managed to find a pair of nutcrackers to replace the old ones, but everything else was still in shambles. She just hadn't had the time—or heart—to deal with the mess.

Rebekah frowned at Grace's sudden change in demeanor, then quickly perked up again. "You know what? This calls for a shopping trip! While we're out, we can stop by the craft store and get supplies to make custom decorations. Before you know it, the place will look even better than it did last year!"

Cole stood again and handed a set of keys to Grace. "Sounds like you'll need my truck to haul everything home." He pulled Grace in for a hug. "Let me know when you're back, and I'll come over and help out."

"You guys are the best," Grace said, smiling at them both. "I've been telling people for a year now that it's not things that matter but the experiences we create with our loved ones. It's time I follow that advice myself." She squeezed Cole's midsection, then let go, smiling up at him one last time. "Thanks for letting us borrow your truck!"

"Anytime. Now go have some fun!" Cole cheered.

***

Grace and Rebekah left the house, two women on a mission to save Christmas...well, to save it for them at least. Not everyone cared as much as Grace did about Christmas trees and decorations.

"You think we can be back by dark?" Grace asked as she hopped into the driver's seat.

Rebekah looked at her watch before hoisting herself into the passenger side. "It's only ten, so there's a reasonable chance. You must be planning to buy more than I thought!"

"You have no idea!" Grace started the truck, backed out, and then headed down Cole's long, winding driveway.

After a few moments of silence, Rebekah turned to Grace and smiled. "Cole must really love you."

"Why do you say that?" Grace asked curiously. She turned onto the main road and did her best to adjust to driving Cole's much larger truck.

"Because men only let women they love drive their trucks!" Rebekah replied with a laugh. "And sometimes not even then."

Grace gave her a sideways glance. "You sound like someone speaking from experience."

"Thorne bought a new truck once he settled in," Rebekah said, "and I swear, that man would give me a kidney before he'd let me drive his baby." She laughed. "And he's not even a truck guy!"

They drove in silence for a few minutes before Grace got up the nerve to ask the question she'd spent the last few days avoiding. "How are things going between you and Thorne?"

Rebekah turned to face Grace, her eyes narrowed in suspicion. "They're fine—why? Do you know something I don't?"

Grace shook her head quickly. "No, nothing like that. It's just...I've been wondering how you're feeling. Seeing Hunter again gave me a better appreciation for the relationship I have with Cole, but my history with Hunter is practically non-existent next to yours. I was wondering how it affected you; that's all."

"I think for me, seeing Hunter again brought closure. At one point, I remember feeling relieved that he was no longer my problem," Rebekah paused, as if in thought. "Not that he's a terrible person—just that it's nice to be in a relationship that doesn't require secrecy or lies."

"I get it," Grace said, nodding. "I mean, I don't have experience with that, but I get what you're saying. I think I have some sort of problem where I need to see everyone paired off and living happily ever after!" She meant that as a joke, but even to her ears, she could tell it didn't come off that way.

Rebekah reached over and took her hand, giving it a squeeze before releasing it. "That's your romantic side talking," she teased. "When people fall in love, they want everyone else to be in love, too. It's a natural response; however, it is possible for people to be single and happy."

"I wasn't," Grace mumbled.

"I'm not sure I was either," Rebekah said, "but I think that had less to do with a lack of a romantic partner and more to do with not living the life I wanted to live. You have a great thing going with Cole, but he isn't the only thing in your life that has changed or brought you happiness." She reached over and squeezed Grace's hand again. "Anyway, thank you for checking in with me; I appreciate the reminder that you care."

Grace smiled at her friend. "Any chance we might be hearing wedding bells in your future?"

"Only the ones I'll be ringing for your wedding," Rebekah joked. "Seriously, though, Thorne and I are taking things slow, and I'm good with that."

They pulled into the parking lot of the home goods store and parked in the back.

When Rebekah shot her a questioning look, Grace shrugged. "It's easier to get out when you park far away from everyone else."

Rebekah laughed. "Fair enough. I need to get my steps in anyway." She pulled a list out of her purse. "I hope you don't mind, but I took the liberty of writing down some things I think we'll need."

"That's great! I wish I had thought to do the same." Grace put the keys in her purse and prepared to get out of the truck. "Are you ready to shop till we drop?"

"Always! Just don't let me get carried away. I am so excited to be celebrating my first real Christmas; I might just buy out the store!"

***

Three hours, four shopping carts, and half a dozen flat carts later, they were back at the truck and struggling to load everything inside.

"It's a good thing Cole let us borrow this bad boy, but I'm starting to think we should have brought a trailer, too," Grace said as she tried to squeeze more bags into the backseat. "I think we might have spent more money than we did last summer when we bought all those mirrors and televisions for the hotel."

Rebekah stopped what she was doing and turned to stare at Grace. "We didn't buy a single decoration for the hotel!" she gasped in horror. She looked around at their purchases with wild eyes. "Please don't tell me we need to go back in there and buy more."

Grace slowly held out her hands as if approaching a wild animal. "It's okay," she said soothingly. "I don't plan to rent out the hotel this time, and at three stories tall, I have no desire to hang lights either."

"How many times have we said that and then ended up renting it out anyway?"

"Fair enough," Grace conceded. "But let's cross that bridge when we get to it. Besides, we couldn't fit another single bulb in here even if we tried, so we're off the hook regardless."

"For now," Rebekah stated.

"Yes, for now." Grace shut the door, then started gathering carts to return to the cart corral. "Can you really say you didn't have fun?"

Rebekah grabbed a couple of the flat carts and followed Grace. "Actually, I had a blast! I can't wait to get home and start decorating. I guess I just got overwhelmed for a second and panicked. Maybe that's why my mom always hired a company to do all the decorating for her."

Grace nodded. "I felt that way last year, but that all changed when the cavalry arrived to help!"

They hopped in the truck and got situated as best they could around the overflow of bags that ended up in the front seat.

"Do you think we'll have a lot of help this year?" Rebekah asked hopefully.

"How about this: while I drive back, you call the pizza place and order half a dozen pies." Grace put the truck in drive and slowly pulled out of the parking lot. "If we feed them, they will come!"

Rebekah pulled her phone out of her purse and scrolled. "After I do that, I'll send out a text to everyone to meet us at the house."

"Sounds good. And you know what? I'll even let you hang the first decoration!"

She clasped her hands together in glee, her phone falling to her lap. "This is so exciting!" She then picked her phone back up and continued scrolling.

Grace smiled at Rebekah's enthusiasm. She may have had to postpone her wedding, but she had a feeling this would still be one of the most magical Christmases she'd ever had.

-Nineteen-

G race was just finishing the breakfast dishes when Molly walked in, baby carrier in hand.

"Hey, Molly, what's up?" Grace asked, surprised to see her friend back so soon. Molly had left after breakfast with Grant, presumably to head to the office.

Molly set the carrier down on the breakfast bar, then took a seat on one of the stools. "I wanted to talk to you," she replied.

Why did those words always sound so ominous? They were only slightly better than their more malevolent cousin, "We need to talk."

"Okay..." Grace hesitated. "Please don't tell me you have more bad news. I'm not sure I can take any more."

"No, no, it's nothing like that," Molly said, waving her hand dismissively. "I just wanted to check in and see how you're feeling, and to tell you that we don't have to do the Christmas Experience if you don't want to. Since Amelia Parrish left a tip after her visit last Thanksgiving that covered our home-repair costs, we're back on track financially."

At the mention of Amelia's name, an image of the woman popped into Grace's head. She still wasn't sure why Amelia had been so generous, but Grace appreciated it all the same. Without her help, things would be a lot harder right now.

"You know what? I think we should move forward with our plans for the Christmas Experience," Grace mused. "I know we technically don't have to, but this past year has been nothing but struggles, and it would be nice to start the new year with a bit of a financial cushion, you know?"

Molly nodded. "That makes sense; it's just... I know you've been dealing with a lot lately, and I don't want to see you get burned out."

Grace smiled at her friend and business partner. "Thank you, I appreciate that. But right now, I'm actually looking forward to hosting another Experience. Last year really was magical, and it would be wonderful to create more of that magic this year—especially since we have so many new friends and family members to celebrate with."

"Okay, then. I guess that's settled." Molly reached over the counter and squeezed Grace's hand. "I'll finalize things with our newest batch of guests this morning, then get the list to you by this evening so you can finish making your plans." When Grace winced, Molly groaned. "You do have plans, right?"

"I have some," Grace said defensively. "It's hard to come up with things to do around here—you know that. And I don't want to repeat last year. Even if all the guests are new, I want everything to feel fresh and exciting."

Molly patted Grace's hand, then stood. "I get that, but just remember: you don't have to reinvent the wheel."

"But isn't that part of the package?" Grace asked.

"No." Molly shook her head as she picked up the baby carrier. "You didn't promise something flashy that's never been done before. You promised a return to the Christmases of our youth—to the way things were before it became all about money and gifts. It's about the experiences people have with their loved ones and the memories they make, remember?"

Grace nodded, then sighed. "You're right, thanks. I need to be careful not to forget why people are coming here. It's just so easy to get caught up in all the glamour and perfection I see on social media. I guess I want to be the Martha Stewart of Christmas!"

"And that is why you leave social media to Rebekah and me," Molly teased. "Seriously, Grace, you're amazing at what you do. You don't need to emulate Martha or anyone else."

"Thanks, Molly. I'll do my best to remember that."

"Good." Molly nodded. "Now say goodbye to baby Eliza; we need to get to work!"

Grace walked around the counter and bent down to kiss little Eliza's cheek. "Bye, baby girl," she whispered to the sleeping infant. Then she stood and hugged Molly. "Are you coming to the council meeting?" she asked as she walked Molly out.

"Not unless you need me to," Molly replied. "I have a ton of work to catch up on. Who knew taking two months off for maternity leave would cause us to get so far behind?"

"Is there anything I can do to help?"

"If I come up with something, I'll let you know. But, girl, you have more than enough to handle on your own!" Molly opened the front door and stepped into the cold. "This is the price we pay for being boss babes!"

Grace laughed. "It's a dirty job, but somebody's gotta do it!"

"Amen!"

***

Despite the cold, Grace decided to walk down to the town hall for the council meeting. She thought fresh air might help clear her head, and since the town hall was only five blocks from her house, it seemed worth the risk of freezing. Two blocks in, she regretted that decision—but she was too stubborn to turn around. So she took off running, hoping the faster pace would warm her up. Winter in the Midwest was a peculiar thing. One day it's sunny and warm; the next, frigid and snowing.

When she finally arrived, she took a seat next to Bea, then looked around at a couple of unfamiliar faces. "Who are these people?" she whispered to Bea.

Bea nodded toward a woman who looked to be around Grace's age. "That's Brynn—she's the owner of the new coffee shop. And that," Bea said, pointing to the woman next to Brynn, "is Lyda. She's also opening a store, but I'm not quite sure what kind."

Interesting, Grace thought. Apparently things were changing in their small town, and she'd been too preoccupied to notice. Although she had seen the coffee shop last month when she and Rebekah walked down Main Street.

"Who's that man?" Grace asked, nodding toward the seat Mayor Allen usually occupied.

"That's Derek Morgan. He's filling in for Mayor Allen while he's away." Bea turned to face Grace. "I just realized..."

"That the wedding is off?" Grace finished for her.

"Postponed," Rebekah said as she dropped into the chair beside Grace. "You can't keep telling people the wedding is off," she admonished. "You're going to give someone a heart attack."

Bea chuckled. "She's right, you know," Bea said, nodding toward Rebekah. "You certainly gave me a start when you said that."

Grace rolled her eyes and crossed her arms over her chest. "Well, that's how it feels," she pouted.

"You know, since the wedding has been postponed, I should be free to make the cake," Bea said.

"Really?" Grace asked in excitement. "Please tell me you're serious." She grabbed Bea's hand and held it tight.

"Of course," Bea laughed. "I always wanted to make it for you; I just couldn't squeeze it in around all the holiday orders." Her face grew serious as she squeezed Grace's hand. "I would be honored to make your wedding cake, honestly."

Grace squealed. "Finally, something has gone right! This is a sign, right?"

Rebekah bumped Grace's shoulder. "Yep—it's definitely a sign. I told you things would work out if we gave them time."

"Ahem." The man Bea had identified as Derek rose and cleared his throat. "If everyone is here, I think it's time to get this meeting started."

He looked around, seeking confirmation that everyone was present. When Junior nodded, Derek proceeded. "For those of you who don't know me, I'm Derek Morgan—Mayor Allen's friend and business partner. He has asked me to fill in for him while he is away tending to personal matters."

"I didn't realize the mayor could temporarily appoint replacements," Grace whispered to Bea. "Shouldn't a council member have been chosen for that role?"

Derek looked at Grace. "Excuse me, ma'am, but did you have a question?"

Grace felt her cheeks heat. She felt like she was back in grade school, getting reprimanded by the teacher for talking during a lesson. Thankfully, Rebekah reached over and took her hand, giving her the courage to speak up. "I was asking why a man who doesn't live here and has no knowledge of our town is now in charge?"

"That sounds like a reasonable question," Derek replied. "May I ask who you are?"

In Grace's opinion, Derek had just proved her point—but she decided against pointing that out. "My name is Grace Parker. I own the local bed and breakfast and part of the hotel."

"I see. And what is it that you're concerned I don't know?"

"Well, I plan to host another Christmas Experience in a couple of weeks, and as those who were here last year know, the town is a big part of that. Since you're in charge, do you plan to offer the same support Mayor Allen always has?"

Derek appeared to consider this. "Since I'm unsure what all that entails, I think it's best if you and I talk about it after the meeting."

"That's fine, but that topic is on today's agenda," Grace argued. "Decorating the town is a huge endeavor, and if we're going to do it, we need to get started right away. Last year, we had daily meetings for weeks to make sure everything was done in time."

"Then I guess the answer is no." Derek's face was a mask of indifference.

Grace sat up straight, panic and fear playing tug-of-war in her chest.

"Excuse me? No what?"

"No, the town will not be participating this year in your little Christmas Experience," he replied without emotion.

"Now wait just a minute," Junior said, his voice rising above the murmurs. "You may be acting mayor, but these matters are up to the council to vote on."

Derek sighed, annoyance replacing indifference. "Fine, go ahead and vote then."

"All in favor say 'aye,'" Junior instructed.

A chorus of "ayes" rang out in response.

"All opposed say 'nay,'" Junior continued.

"Nay," Derek said loudly. He looked around the room, but no one else sided with him. "I never should have agreed to this," he mumbled. "Fine. Grace, I'll see you after the meeting. Are there any other items on the agenda?"

Bea raised her hand, stood, and addressed the group. "I would have preferred to do this when Allen was here, but here goes." She closed her eyes, took a deep breath, and opened them again. "After much deliberation, I have made the difficult decision to close Bea's Bakery, effective January 1st."

Grace gasped, covering her mouth. "Oh my gosh!" Bea's Bakery—and Bea herself—had been a fixture in Winterwood for as long as she could remember. Losing the bakery would be a huge blow to the community, as well as to Grace personally.

"Don't worry, darlin', I will still make your wedding cake," Bea assured her. "In fact, it'll be the last thing I make as a professional baker."

Tears sprang to Grace's eyes, but she did her best to hold them back. This meeting was supposed to be about bringing the town to life for Christmas. Instead, she'd suffered not one but two blows from Derek and Bea. There were too many changes happening, and she didn't like it one bit.

"Anyone else have something to say?" Derek asked. When no one replied, he sighed and shook his head. "Meeting adjourned."

Grace slumped in her seat, still gripping Rebekah's hand. "This is just awful," she whined. "And why do I feel like I was just called to the principal's office?"

"Because, in a way, you were," Rebekah teased. "At least he's handsome," she pointed out.

"How does that help?" Grace asked, studying Derek. He was kind of handsome if you liked the surfer look: tousled sandy-blonde hair, blue eyes, and a lean, toned build—like he belonged on the cover of Surfer Magazine.

"I don't know," Rebekah said. "I've always heard you're supposed to imagine people in their underwear when you're nervous," she added with a shrug.

Bea and Grace exchanged looks. "I thought that was for when you're giving a speech in public?" Bea asked.

"It doesn't matter," Grace interrupted. "Please tell me you're coming with me so I don't have to face him alone?"

"I'm sorry, darlin', but I have to get back to work," Bea said apologetically. "But if he gives you any trouble, just let Junior know and he'll take care of it."

Grace continued to pout. "I don't know what's worse: having to deal with Derek or losing the bakery."

"Dear girl, I'm not leaving the country; I'm just retiring," Bea said. "I've been getting up at four o'clock every morning for the better part of four decades. I'm tired, I'm old, and I just don't have it in me anymore."

"I understand," Grace said softly, though she really didn't. For over twenty years, things had been almost exactly the same in Winterwood. Now, all of a sudden, everything was changing. Why now? She turned to Rebekah. "Please tell me you're at least coming with me?"

Rebekah gently pried her hand from Grace's grasp and gave her a side hug. "Of course. I won't abandon you to the sharks, but I do wish Molly were here. Derek wouldn't stand a chance against her."

Grace raised an eyebrow. "Aren't you supposed to be New York tough?"

"That was the old Rebekah," she said with a laugh. "The new Rebekah is trying to be a little more diplomatic."

"Good luck, ladies," Bea said with a chuckle. "I'm sure it won't be anywhere near as bad as you fear."

Grace watched Bea leave, then turned to Rebekah. "Might as well get this over with." She stood and lead the way to the mayor's office. She'd seen Derek make a beeline for it as soon as the meeting ended and wondered why Mayor Allen had chosen him as replacement. Not that Allen wanted to stick around any longer than he had to, but at least he knew everyone. Derek didn't know a soul. Nor did he seem to care.

When they reached the office, they knocked once and then opened the door. Derek had his back turned, phone to his ear. After a few moments of silence, he said "Goodbye," and tossed his phone onto the desk. He then looked up, saw the two of them, and jumped as if startled by their appearance.

"Didn't your mom teach you how to knock?" he asked angrily.

"No, she died before she could," Grace deadpanned.

Derek's mouth opened and closed a few times before he nervously cleared his throat. "I...uh...I'm sorry to hear that. Now, if you don't mind, I have some business to attend to. Can we reschedule this for tomorrow morning?"

"Sure," Grace replied. That would give her plenty of time to obsess over the meeting and imagine every worst-case scenario possible. It would also give her time to convince Molly to come along, so basically, a win–win.

Grace followed Rebekah out of the building and over to Rebekah's car. "That was weird," Grace said as soon as they were out of earshot of anyone who'd been at the meeting.

"Yes, it was," Rebekah agreed. "I wonder what's really going on with Derek?"

"If there's anyone who would know, it's—"

"Gladys!" they said in unison.

-Eighteen-

Just like with Derek, Grace and Rebekah had to wait until that morning to talk to Gladys. Their friend had spent the previous afternoon at a doctor's appointment and then been too tired to come for dinner, which worried Grace almost as much as the mayor's meeting had. Gladys wasn't getting any younger, and—just as with Granny—it was starting to show.

As Grace busied herself with getting breakfast on the table, her friends filed into the dining room and took their seats. Once everyone had been served, Grace sat between Rebekah and Molly and turned to Gladys.

"Please tell me everything you know about the acting mayor," Grace pleaded.

Gladys chuckled and lifted her coffee cup. "Already causing trouble, is he?" she asked, raising a brow.

Grace nodded emphatically. "We just met him yesterday, and he's already tried to cancel the town's decorations."

Surprise crossed Gladys's face. "Hmm. I expected him to be difficult, but not that difficult." When the rest of them stared at her, she continued. "Derek grew up here.

If I remember correctly, he graduated high school right before you started, Grace."

"If he's local, why have I never met him?" Grace asked. Given how much of a recluse she'd been since dropping out of college to care for Granny, it was a bit of a foolish question—but you'd think she'd have seen him around at least once last year. Handsome, eligible men tended to stick out in a town this size, and she hadn't noticed a ring...

"He left town right after high school, and to my knowledge, hasn't been back since. Some time in the last ten years, he became a partner in Allen's real estate business. Derek handles all of their clients in the city, while Allen focuses on Winterwood and the smaller surrounding towns."

That made sense. What didn't make sense was why Derek had come back only to immediately antagonize the town. "Does he hate Winterwood?" Grace asked, her concern growing with each new piece of information.

"I'm not sure," Gladys replied, taking another sip of coffee as she gazed out the window. "His parents split up right before he left town. It's possible he just doesn't want to deal with the memories."

Grace's heart went out to him. She could imagine how hard that must have been, and she sympathized—returning after all those years would be difficult. Still, she couldn't let him play Scrooge and ruin Christmas. It did mean adjusting her approach. *Ugh! Why was everything always so complicated?*

"Did he succeed in canceling the decorations?" Molly asked, frowning.

Grace shook her head. "No. Junior insisted on a vote, and the council outvoted him."

Molly nodded, determination on her face. "Good. At least we have the council's support."

A ding sounded, and everyone glanced around for the source.

"It's me," Rebekah said, holding up her phone. She read the message, then turned to Grace apologetically. "I'm so sorry, but Kenzie just sent an S.O.S. and I need to get out to the winery ASAP."

"It's okay," Grace said. "I'm a big girl. I can handle meeting Derek alone."

Rebekah looked past Grace at Molly. "Could you go with her?"

Molly shook her head. "I wish I could, but I have back-to-back meetings all morning."

"Anyone else available?" Rebekah asked.

Grant and Emilio shook their heads, but Gladys and Granny exchanged intrigued looks.

"I can go," Gladys announced. She turned to Granny. "How about you, Josie? Up for a little adventure?"

"I think these old bones can handle the trip!" Granny reached over and patted Grace's hand.

"Y'all do realize I literally just said I'd be fine, right?" Grace rolled her eyes and sighed when they all nodded and smiled. "Whatever. We need to leave as soon as we finish breakfast. Will you two be ready?"

Gladys eyed Granny's neatly pressed slacks and freshly laundered sweater. "We look ready to me."

"Now I wish I could go," Rebekah joked. "Poor Derek won't know what hit him when these two show up," she added, nodding toward Granny and Gladys.

"We should have been her first choice, anyway," Gladys sniffed.

Baby Eliza began to cry, mercifully sparing Grace from more conversation. Never one to waste an opportunity, Grace stood and cleared the breakfast plates. By the time she finished, everyone except Granny and Gladys had left.

"Guess it's just us now," Grace said. "Are you ready?"

"Of course, dear," Granny replied. "Just let me grab my coat."

Grace grabbed her jacket, purse, and car keys. "I'll pull the car around and meet you out front."

Without waiting for a reply, she knelt to give Piper and Ruby goodbye pets—only to remember they were still at Cole's. Would she ever get used to bouncing between the farm and the house? She shook her head. That was a problem for another day. Right now, she needed to focus on Derek, the Scrooge intent on ruining Christmas.

***

Grace, Granny, and Gladys entered the town hall and approached the mayor's office.

"Hi, Katie," Grace said to the town manager/receptionist. "We're here to see Derek."

Katie rolled her eyes and smirked. "He's in there," she said, nodding toward the office door. She leaned forward conspiratorially. "Just so you know, he's not in a good mood."

"Thanks for the warning," Grace replied. Derek had been in a bad mood yesterday, too. Was he ever in a good mood?

When they reached the door, Grace remembered his lecture about knocking and rapped loudly and firmly. A moment later, he called, "Come in!" She opened the door and stepped inside, Granny and Gladys right behind her.

"Rather petty, don't you think?" he asked dryly.

"What's petty?" Grace said, feigning innocence.

Derek opened his mouth to respond, then glanced past Grace and saw Gladys and Granny standing behind her. "Can I help you two?" he asked.

"Yes, you can, young man," Granny replied. "You can start by telling me why you're treating my granddaughter so poorly."

"Oh, wow, you brought your grandmother to our meeting?" Derek asked, turning to Granny. "Look, ma'am, I'm not treating anyone poorly. I'm just doing my job. When Allen asked me to step in, he made it sound like I'd be a glorified office sitter for a few weeks. At no point did he mention I'd have to turn Winterwood into Santa's Village."

"And I take it you would have declined if he'd told you that?" Gladys asked, arching an eyebrow.

Derek picked up a pen and clicked it relentlessly. "Well, yes," he admitted grudgingly. "But it's unfair to make it sound like that's a bad thing. I'm busy; I don't have time for this. Nor do I, frankly, care."

Grace sucked in a sharp breath. "You don't care about Christmas?"

"For Pete's sake," he sighed, rubbing his eyes. "Can we focus on the task at hand?"

"Which is?" Grace asked, bewildered by his tone.

He clicked his pen again. "Since I have no choice, what exactly needs to happen to fulfill the decorating obligation?"

"Oh, well," Grace said, exhaling. "Last year, we held daily meetings at 7:00 a.m. at Addie's restaurant. Mayor Allen led them and made sure every committee had enough volunteers so all tasks got done."

"Could you say that again, in English please?" he asked, dropping the pen on the desk and pressing his face into his hands. "Why did I agree to this?" he muttered to himself.

Grace drew in a steadying breath. This was going worse than she'd feared. "Okay, look, all I need you to do is show up at the tree-lighting ceremony and plug in the Christmas lights. I'll handle everything else. Can you do that?"

"Don't you need a man to back you up and keep order?" he asked.

"I'm going to pretend you didn't say that," Grace replied through gritted teeth.

Derek surprised her by grinning. "Go ahead and add 'chauvinistic pig' to my list of crimes," he drawled.

"I will assume we have an agreement," Grace said. "But, Mr. Morgan, you might want to be careful—before you get visited by three ghosts."

"Ha, ha, very funny," he said sarcastically. "I consider Scrooge a mentor, so I take that as a compliment."

"I don't think I've heard anything sadder in my life," Granny said quietly. "And I've lived a long time."

Derek shifted uncomfortably and began clicking his pen again. "If that's all, feel free to show yourselves out."

The three women turned to leave, with Grace bringing up the rear.

"Grace," Derek called out. "I'd like to talk to you for a minute—*alone.*"

It was tempting to ignore him, but if she wanted any chance of a working relationship, she needed to appear cooperative. She handed her keys to Gladys. "Go ahead and wait in the car. I'll be right there."

"Are you sure?" Gladys asked, taking the keys reluctantly.

"Absolutely," Grace replied with a smile.

Once they were gone, Grace closed the door and took a seat in front of Derek. "What do you want?"

"It's not very professional to bring your grandmother to a business meeting," he said reproachfully.

"I run a bed and breakfast, not a corporation," she replied with a shrug. "Besides, Granny owns the house I use for my business, so she has every right to be here."

Derek considered that. "Fair enough," he conceded. "I just don't appreciate you turning half the town against me."

"I haven't turned anyone against you," Grace replied. "You're the one who chose to come into town and start dismantling long-held traditions."

"Pfft," he snorted. "Who are you kidding? We both know this town was dead before you decided to revive it last year."

Grace clenched her fists. "It wasn't dead, just, dormant," she said defensively. "You have no idea how quickly people here banded together. What they created was pure magic."

"Sure, sure," he waved a hand dismissively. "Next you'll tell me the real Santa appeared and Tiny Tim tossed his crutches aside?" He slammed his pen down in frustration. "C'mon, Grace, this is real life, not some Hallmark movie."

No matter what she said, she wouldn't get through to him; that much was obvious. What wasn't obvious was why. "What's your problem? I already gave you an out. What more do you want?"

Derek stared at her, then looked down. "I see you're engaged," he said abruptly, shifting the topic. "Who's the lucky guy?"

It took her a moment to process the abrupt change of topic, but she evetually answered. "Cole Reed."

"The cowboy?" Derek asked, surprised.

"Yes," Grace replied, defensively. "Do you know him?" She wouldn't be surprised if Derek thought Cole was out of her league—she was about to marry him, and she still thought that, too.

"We went to school together," Derek said. "He was a couple of years ahead of me—into 4-H, while I was into football. Even then, you didn't mess with him."

Grace didn't know how to respond to that, so she said nothing. "I'm starting the daily meetings tomorrow morning," she said. "You're welcome to join, but as of now, I'll assume you won't be there."

"I'll see how I feel in the morning," he said cryptically.

"Great. Well, I'll see you," she replied. She grabbed her purse and stood, giving him one last look before leaving. He might be trouble, but if she could handle a mob of elderly protesters, a wedding saboteur, her ex-boyfriend's girlfriend, and her fiancé's ex-wife, surely she could handle an interim mayor with a chip on his shoulder. Right?

-Seventeen-

G race opened the door to Addie's Diner at 6:45 a.m. and instantly froze at the sight. Everywhere she looked were people, and there did not appear to be an inch of standing room left. How was it possible there was an even bigger turnout than last year? More importantly, was it too late for her to turn around and go back home?

"Ahem," came a female voice from behind.

Startled, Grace let go of the door and spun around. "Oh, sorry, you scared me." It was still dark this early, so she struggled to see exactly who she was addressing, but she thought she recognized the woman Bea had referred to as Lyda. "I'm Grace," she said, holding out her hand.

"Lyda Gates," the woman replied. She shook Grace's hand, her grip firm and confident. "I'm here for the meeting," she added, gesturing toward the restaurant entrance.

"Me too," Grace said. "Actually, I'm supposed to be leading it, but I wasn't prepared for the size of the crowd. It's a madhouse in there."

"Ah, I understand," Lyda replied. "Allow me." She stepped past Grace into the diner, shoulders back, head held high.

Grace watched in awe as the crowd seemed to part for Lyda, then hurried after her. When they reached the front of the room, Lyda grabbed a spoon and a glass from a nearby table and clinked them together until the room fell silent. She then stepped aside and motioned for Grace to take the floor. It felt so surreal that Grace pinched herself to make sure she wasn't dreaming.

"Thank you," Grace said to Lyda. When Lyda nodded, Grace turned to the crowd. "Welcome to our first meeting, everyone!"

A chorus of cheers erupted in response.

What a lively bunch, she thought. "For those of you who are new, let me explain how this will work. The council members and I have drafted sign-up sheets for all the tasks we need to complete over the next ten days. Please choose which tasks you'd like to help with and enter your name on the corresponding sheet. The person in charge of each task will contact you later today to arrange a time to go over the details. Any questions?"

Lyda raised her hand. "I'm sure some tasks are more desirable than others. Do you have a plan for handling the more unpopular tasks?"

That was a good question—one Grace didn't remember being a problem last year. "If we end up with tasks that don't have enough volunteers, I will address that at tomorrow's meeting." Grace wondered if that answer was good enough. She studied Lyda's expression and relaxed when Lyda seemed satisfied.

"Any other questions?" Grace asked the crowd.

"What events will the town hold this year?" came a voice from the back.

Another good question, and she didn't have an answer ready. Last year, they'd done a Breakfast with Santa, a festival ending with the tree-lighting ceremony, a parade, and fireworks. Would it be okay to repeat those? Grace supposed she was about to find out.

"We had a great turnout for last year's events, so I'd like to do those again," Grace replied. "However, if anyone has new ideas, I'm open to suggestions." She scanned the room for raised hands and saw Conor waving at her. "Yes, Conor?"

Conor cleared his throat. "The drama club is working on a production of *A Christmas Carol*, and we'd love to make that part of the plans."

"Okay—what do you need from me?" Grace asked, pulling out her phone to jot down a note.

"Specific dates and times, for starters," he said. "Since this is my first year, I have no idea what to expect."

That made two of them. A high school play would be something for her guests to enjoy, so she was happy to help. "Let's talk after the meeting and put together a plan."

"What's the theme for this year?" called a second voice.

Oh, shoot. Mr. Acting Mayor had ended yesterday's meeting so quickly they hadn't nailed down those details. Since everyone still had last year's decorations—well, she assumed they did—she decided to reuse the theme. So much for making things fresh and exciting.

"I think we should stick with Santa's Village," Grace replied. "Next year we can start earlier and discuss new themes then."

Grace tensed as the crowd murmured. Were they unhappy with that? How would she handle complaints? Why had she volunteered to lead these meetings in the first place?

A hand on her arm drew her attention away from the panic. "Breathe," Lyda whispered in her ear.

Grace took a deep breath and turned back to the crowd. "Anyone else?" When no one spoke up, she retrieved the stack of sign-up sheets and passed them to the council members seated in the front row. "Please remember to sign up before you leave. Thank you so much for coming." Grace looked around at all the familiar—and not-so-familiar—faces. "I'll see you all tomorrow!"

Before she could process what was happening, Lyda grabbed her hand and dragged her through the throng and out the door into the parking lot.

"Thanks," Grace said, bending over to catch her breath. "I'm sure you saw how awful I was at that."

"Nonsense, you did fine," Lyda replied. "You just need to project more confidence, that's all."

That's all? Grace thought. People always said that as if it were easy. But for them, maybe it was.

"That was quite the turnout in there," Derek said as he exited the diner. "Just so you know, the town will not be paying for that."

Grace's brow furrowed. "Paying for what?"

Derek rolled his eyes. "I really do have to explain everything to you, don't I?" He sighed. "We will not pay for the food and drink consumed during the meeting."

"Okaaayyy," Grace drawled. "I don't recall asking you to."

"Good, then we're clear."

The urge to roll her eyes was strong, but she resisted. "Why are you even here? I thought we agreed your presence wasn't necessary."

"I never agreed to anything," he replied. "As acting mayor, it's my job to make sure the rest of you do yours. So here I am, making sure you did your job this morning."

"I don't work for you," Grace reminded him. "You have zero control over what I do. You, on the other hand, answer to the council—a fact you might want to remember before you throw your weight around again."

"Pfft," he snorted. "You act as if I even want this job. Newsflash: I don't. I'm only here because Allen asked me to and—"

Lyda stepped between them. "How about we all take a breather before someone says something they'll regret?" she interrupted. "We're on the same team here, okay?"

"I'm not sure I believe that," Grace replied. "But you're right, we don't have time for arguing. If you'll excuse me, I need to go home and get to work." She spun on her heel and headed to her car.

Grace could not remember a time when someone got under her skin as badly as Derek did. Not even Valerie or

Rebekah had managed to irritate her as much as him. She'd just have to do better. What other choice did she have?

***

After breakfast, Grace texted Conor and confirmed their meeting in the high school auditorium after school. Since she had time to kill, she headed out to Cole's, hopeful for some quality time with him. When she arrived, she found him in the barn brushing out a horse.

"Hey there, handsome," she said, wrapping her arms around his waist from behind.

Cole stopped brushing, turned, and pulled her into his arms. "Good morning, gorgeous," he whispered against her ear. "How did the meeting go?"

Grace sighed and hugged him tighter. "It went fine until Derek showed up and started an argument. I swear, that guy has it out for me, and I have no idea why."

"I'm sorry, darlin'; it sounds like I should have been there," Cole said.

"No," Grace pulled back to look up at him. "We are not disrupting your busy schedule over this. It's my problem; I will deal with it."

"Your problems are my problems, baby girl," Cole replied. "But who is this Derek guy?"

They walked back to the house together, arms around each other, trying to stay warm.

"His name is Derek Morgan," Grace explained. "For reasons I don't understand, Mayor Allen named him interim mayor while he's away on family business." She looked up at Cole. "He claims he went to high school with you and said you were 'someone not to be messed with'—whatever that means."

Cole smiled and furrowed his brow. "I have no idea what that's supposed to mean, but if it's the guy I think it is, I'm not surprised by his attitude."

"So you do know him?"

"I wouldn't say I know him," Cole replied. "He was a couple of years behind me. I did know of him: Derek was a gifted football player—already on the varsity team as a sophomore, which isn't common. Word around town was that scouts were offering full rides to some of the bigger-named colleges."

Grace tried to process that. She knew next to nothing about football scouts or scholarships, but she wondered how a guy went from that to a career in real-estate. "What do you think happened?"

"What do you mean?"

"If he was that gifted, why isn't he in the NFL or something?" She was genuinely curious and wondered if the answer would provide a clue to Derek's current attitude.

Cole opened the door to the house and led Grace inside. "I have no idea, darlin'. Like I said, we weren't friends. Once I graduated and started working the farm full-time, I barely had time to keep up with the people I was friends with, let alone ones I wasn't."

Grace walked to the fireplace and bent down to pet Max and Ruby, who were snuggled in their beds in front of the fire. "Who's a good boy and girl?" she asked as they soaked up the attention. When she finished, she went to the couch and sat down. Moments later, Piper jumped into Grace's lap, and Grace hugged the little fur ball to her chest, much to Piper's chagrin.

"I'm pretty sure they missed you as much as you missed them," Cole said as he sat beside her.

"I miss all of you when I'm not here," she said. "But I think you're right to keep them here instead of dragging them back and forth all the time."

Cole wrapped his arm around her shoulders and pulled her close. "You didn't have to leave," he whispered against her hair.

"I didn't want to," she admitted. "But I didn't know what else to do. Granny seemed eager to go home, and it felt wrong to keep her here against her will."

"Someday soon we'll have to talk about that," he reminded her. "I really don't want to live separately from my wife."

"Nor I from my husband," she replied. She wrapped her arms around his neck and kissed him, wanting him to know how much she loved him. When they pulled apart, she rested her head on his shoulder.

Moments like these kept her going; moments where everything felt right, even when it wasn't. "Not to change the subject—though that's exactly what I'm doing—but I still don't understand why Mayor Allen chose Derek to replace him. Why pick a guy who hates Christmas to stand in for you during Christmas?"

"Maybe that's exactly why he chose him," Cole said.

"What do you mean?"

"I mean, maybe Allen hoped your Christmas spirit would work its magic on Derek."

"*My* Christmas spirit?" she asked, raising a brow.

"Yes, *yours*," Cole replied. He pulled her back until they were lying on the couch, then draped a blanket over them. "We'll talk about this after our nap."

She snuggled into him, head on his chest. "Since when do you take naps?" she teased.

"Since it's cold outside and warm in here," he said, eyes already closed, his hat pulled over his face.

Grace giggled, then melted when Piper curled up in a ball on Cole's chest. *My little family*, she thought. She didn't have time for a nap—with only ten days to go until her guests arrived—but she decided to make some time. Once things got hectic, moments like these would be rare, so she'd better enjoy them while she could.

***

Grace rushed to the high school auditorium. She had napped much longer than she expected and was now running late to meet Conor. She'd be lying if she said it wasn't worth it, but being late stressed her out, and she was already stressed.

Since school was out, she didn't have to sign in at the office and was able to head straight to the auditorium, which was a huge relief. She liked Gwen, the school secretary, but today she couldn't afford small talk. Grace winced at the thought—she felt so snobby—and was immediately grateful no one could hear her thoughts. She couldn't remember ever feeling this way before, and the only thing that had changed was her interactions with Derek. He was getting to her more than she realized.

"I am so sorry I'm late," she said to Conor once she found him.

"It's no problem," Conor replied, grinning. "I just finished getting the kids settled, so this is actually perfect timing."

Well, that was a relief. "What did you want to talk about?" Grace asked, glancing at a group of teens assembling a Victorian London–style backdrop onstage.

"Simply put, how many shows should we do?"

How was she supposed to know that? She knew her guests would want tickets, but she had no idea how many people would attend a high school play. Since he expected an answer, she offered her best guess. "Comparable to the number of shows you put on at Easter."

"Okay," Conor said, nodding as he thought it over. "I was thinking it would be cool to do something special on Christmas Eve, like an extra performance. Any thoughts?"

Last year, she and her guests had gone caroling on Christmas Eve and handed out food boxes to elderly and disabled townsfolk. She'd love to repeat that, but on a bigger scale. "What if, after the performance, Santa appears and hands out presents? We could coordinate it with the Breakfast with Santa event, so Santa would already know what they wanted."

Conor's mouth opened and closed a few times as he processed the idea. "I don't know, Grace, that sounds like a lot to coordinate so quickly. Plus, where would the money come from? I was hoping the play itself could raise some funds for the drama club, and even then, I wasn't expecting much."

"I suppose you're right," Grace admitted. "It would be especially tricky if kids asked for expensive electronics or ponies or whatever it is they want these days. Never mind, stupid idea."

"It's not stupid; I'm just not sure it's feasible," Conor said kindly.

Grace smiled. "That's a polite way of saying I'm crazy! But what if the kids stayed in costume and went caroling after the play? I know the families we plan to visit would love that."

"That sounds a lot more doable," Conor teased. "Thanks, Grace. I'll start working on permission slips now, hopefully the kids return them before winter break."

"When you sell tickets, make it donation-only. You can suggest an amount, but people tend to be more generous that way, especially when they know it's for a good cause."

Conor fell into step beside her as they left the auditorium. "Got it, thanks!"

Since her work there was done, Grace waved goodbye and headed to her car. It was time to check in with the rest of the council and see how sign-ups went. If she was lucky, Lyda's earlier concerns would already be a distant memory. If she was lucky—though, given how things had gone so far, she wasn't holding her breath.

-Sixteen-

G race crossed the parking lot in a sleep-deprived daze. Despite her nap the previous day, she felt utterly exhausted. It was likely due to all the running around she'd been doing, but knowing why she was tired did nothing to ease her actual fatigue.

She was just reaching for the door handle when another hand reached out at the same time. Startled, Grace looked up to see an equally exhausted Lyda. "We need to stop meeting like this," Grace joked.

Lyda shook her head as if to clear the fog from her brain. "Oh, good morning," she said sleepily. "Forgive me, I wasn't paying attention."

"I wasn't either," Grace admitted. "If we're this exhausted by day two, I'm scared to see what the rest of the days will look like."

"What?" Lyda asked, confused. "Oh, you mean the Christmas stuff. Sorry, I have a little one sick at home and got absolutely no sleep last night. I probably shouldn't even be here, but if I'm going to be part of this town, I want to do my part."

The words "little one" stuck out in Grace's mind. She realized just how little she knew about the woman. Lyda had seemed so familiar that Grace had forgotten they were practically strangers. "I should give you my phone number," Grace offered. "That way you can call or text me for updates and you don't have to come to all these meetings."

"I will gladly accept your number, but I don't mind coming," Lyda replied. "It's nice to see all the residents show up to support our town. Things have changed since I last lived here; in a good way."

That was news to Grace. Lyda did seem a bit older than her, but it still felt odd that they'd lived in the same town and never met, especially in a town the size of Winterwood. Grace must have been more of a recluse than she thought.

"Ladies," Derek called as he strode toward them, "it's time for the meeting, is it not?"

Grace turned to face the man who'd become a thorn in her side. "Shall I assume your presence means you plan to lead the meeting?"

"Nope," he replied. "Just here to make sure you don't get carried away."

"I thought you claimed you were too busy for this?" Grace reminded him.

Derek shrugged. "I rearranged my schedule."

"I'm sure you did," Grace said sweetly. "Now, if you'll excuse me, I have a meeting to run." She walked off before he could reply—only slightly annoyed when he followed her to the front of the room.

The crowd was smaller today, but she wasn't surprised; most people had already been assigned tasks the day before. These meetings were mostly status updates.

Lyda, who had also followed Grace to the front, clinked a spoon and glass until the room was once again quiet.

"Good morning," Grace called. "I want to start by giving a huge 'thank you' to everyone who signed up to help. We literally could not do this without you."

The audience applauded. Once the clapping died down, Grace continued, "We're set to begin decorating today, and as far as I know, you should already be assigned to groups based on your availability. Does anyone have questions?"

A woman in the back stood and asked, "We'll be decorating the entire downtown area, right?"

Grace nodded. "Yes."

"Does that include the old hotel?" the woman asked. "It wasn't decorated last year, and it stuck out like a sore thumb."

Dang it, she was right. That meant Grace would have to decorate the hotel herself. Even worse, she'd have to find decorations that matched what the rest of Main Street had. How on earth was she supposed to do that on top of everything else?

"I'll make sure it gets done," Grace said through gritted teeth. "Anyone else have a question?" When no one raised their hand, she sighed with relief. "All right, then, I will see you tomorrow. Thanks, everyone!"

For the second day in a row, Lyda grabbed Grace's hand and guided her through the throng of people. Once outside in the parking lot, Lyda paused. "If I'd realized these meetings would be so quick, I would've taken you up on your offer to text me."

"Things are a bit easier this year," Grace explained. "I'm not sure these meetings are even necessary, but I want people to know I'm available. Besides, it's good to remind folks that someone is in charge, otherwise, chaos ensues."

"Makes sense," Lyda said, nodding. "So, if you don't mind my asking, what's the deal with you and the mayor? Did I just witness a meet-cute gone wrong?"

Grace studied Lyda to see if she was joking, but couldn't tell. "Absolutely not. Not only am I engaged to the most wonderful man on the planet, I can't imagine ever dating someone who hates Christmas. So if you're interested, he's all yours."

"As a single mother of two young boys, I think I'll pass," Lyda said with a laugh. "My kids love Christmas, and besides, I can't imagine a man like Derek would choose to be a stepfather."

Hmm, Grace couldn't help but notice Lyda hadn't denied an attraction. She didn't understand what Lyda saw in Derek, but they say there's someone for everyone. "You never know," Grace replied. It wasn't much of a reply, but it was all she had. "Anyway, I hope your son feels better soon."

"Thanks," Lyda said with a curt nod. "If you need help with anything, let me know. I'm free most days when the kids are in school."

They exchanged numbers before Grace remembered something Bea had said. "Aren't you opening a business downtown?" she asked.

"Yes, but that's still some ways off," Lyda replied. "I got one of the old buildings for a song and a dance, but it needs tons of repairs before I can move in." She sighed. "I still plan to decorate it to match the rest of the town, but my grand opening is on hold indefinitely."

"I'm sorry to hear that," Grace said, empathy in her voice. "What kind of business will it be?"

Lyda's face lit up. "Promise not to laugh?"

Grace nodded. "I promise."

"I plan to open a custom hat shop."

Grace didn't feel like laughing—she was just struggling to understand.

"I know, I know, it's crazy, right? A custom hat shop in downtown Winterwood. But I'm doing it as a tribute to my great-grandmother. She opened the first hat shop in the county almost a hundred years ago."

That meant Lyda's family had been here almost as long as Grace's, which made it even stranger they'd never met before. "No offense," Grace said gently, "but do you think you'll get a lot of business here?"

"Absolutely not. But I do have a strong online store that ships worldwide," Lyda explained, smiling as Grace looked confused. "I don't need a storefront, but having a space to make my creations—without a couple of rambunctious boys trampling over them at all hours—would be nice. Plus, people tend to trust businesses more when they have a brick-and-mortar location. Even if a customer never steps inside my shop, I'll still be better off than I am now."

"Well, my B&B is always looking to partner with local businesses, so I'm sure we can make something happen when you're ready," Grace said. She still didn't quite know what to make of a hat shop, but she'd help however she could. Besides, it was nice to see another empty building come to life.

Grace checked her watch. "I need to go, but please text me if you need anything."

"I will," Lyda replied.

They waved goodbye and headed to their cars. When Grace reached hers, she realized they'd been talking for quite some time, and Derek hadn't appeared. That could only mean the townsfolk had detained him. Grace allowed herself a moment to cackle at his misfortune, then drove home to start her morning chores.

***

Breakfast was livelier than usual. Vanessa had surprised everyone by tagging along with her husband, Emilio, bringing their group count to eight. Grace, having grown up eating most meals alone, embraced a 'the more the merrier' attitude when it came to guests.

Unfortunately, it didn't take long for everyone to run off, leaving Grace and Vanessa to clean up the mess.

"So," Grace said while clearing dishes, "how was Thanksgiving with the in-laws?"

Vanessa finished clearing the table and sat at the breakfast bar. "I can't believe I'm about to say this, but it was even weirder than I expected— and I was expecting it to be really weird."

"Oh no, are they still refusing to accept you?" Grace asked, thinking back to Vanessa and Emilio's Halloween wedding. Once Vanessa announced her pregnancy, Emilio's parents had backed down, but before that, they'd been determined to stop the wedding.

"That's just it," Vanessa said, shredding a napkin. "They were the complete opposite this time. His mother wouldn't let me lift a finger the entire visit. It was all 'the baby this' and 'the baby that.' She acted like if I so much as poured a glass of juice, I'd harm the baby." She shook her head. "It was exhausting."

Grace finished loading the dishwasher, then wiped down the counters. "I can only imagine," she said empathetically. "But it sounds like she came from a good place—even if it was annoying."

"That made it worse," Vanessa moaned. "I couldn't complain without sounding like an ungrateful jerk." She watched Grace tidy up the napkin scraps. "And here I am, sitting idly by while you clean up after me."

"If you want something to do, I am more than happy to give you a job," Grace teased.

Vanessa's eyes lit up. "Really? I would love something to do." She laughed when she saw Grace's expression. "Seriously, today is my day off, and after weeks of being waited on hand and foot, I want to prove I'm useful."

"In that case, I need to shop for decorations for the hotel," Grace said. "Any chance you'd like to come with me?"

"Absolutely!" Vanessa replied. "We can use Emilio's SUV, unless you think that won't be big enough?"

Would it be big enough? Grace was fairly certain she could stick to lights, wreaths, and maybe a blow-up snowman or two. It wouldn't match the rest of the town, but it would complement it. After a quick look at downtown that morning, she'd concluded she'd never match the decorations the other businesses had purchased decades ago. It was futile to try.

"Yes, I think that should work," Grace said. "And if it doesn't, we can always strap boxes to the roof."

The doorbell rang, interrupting their conversation.

Vanessa hopped up. "I'll get that, it's probably Emilio checking on me."

Grace watched her go, curious as to who it could be. These days, none of her friends rang the bell if they knew she was home. Moments later, Derek stormed into the kitchen, waving an envelope like a madman.

"It was you, wasn't it?" he yelled.

"Dude, calm down," Grace shouted back, stepping away from him and grabbing her phone. "What was me?"

He thrust the envelope at her, waving it in her face until she took it.

Curious rather than scared, she opened it to find a card. On the front was a ghost illustration and the words Ghost of Christmas Past. Inside were several high-school photos of Derek and a note: If you don't learn from your mistakes, you're doomed to repeat them.

Grace looked up. "You think I sent this to you?"

Vanessa walked over, took the card, gave it a once-over, then handed it back. "This isn't something Grace would do," she said confidently.

"Yeah, right," he spat angrily. "You expect me to believe it's just a coincidence you made a joke about the 'three ghosts,' and now I get this?" He waved the card again for emphasis.

Grace took a deep breath and faced him. "I realize it's a huge coincidence, but I assure you I didn't send that. What would I gain? I have neither the time nor the inclination to mess with you. And where would I have gotten those pictures?"

Derek glared at the photos as he flipped through them. "I don't know, maybe you got them from the school or something?"

"Again, I'd have to ask what I'd gain from that." Grace replied. "Fighting with you makes my life harder, not easier."

"Ah-ha! There's your motive," he exclaimed triumphantly. "You're trying to scare me off so I'll leave town, and then you can do whatever you want. Well, guess what, it isn't going to work!"

Grace narrowed her eyes as he gloated. "Wait, how do I know you didn't send it to yourself to frame me? If anyone has access to those pictures, it's you."

Derek snorted and crossed his arms. "Bold of you to assume I care about you enough to stoop that low."

"Bold of you to assume I care about you," Grace shot back. "Unlike you, I have a real business to run. This isn't some hobby or side quest to fill the hours while my partner is away. This is my life. Honestly, I have far more important things to do than deal with an arrogant, self-obsessed jerk." She grabbed his arm and guided him toward the front door. "I'm sorry someone is targeting you, but it isn't me. So focus on the rest of the people you've ticked off, unless the list is so big it's impossible."

"This isn't over," Derek sneered as he stepped onto the porch.

"Yes, it is," Grace said firmly. She shut the door in his face and locked it so he couldn't come back. She breathed deeply, then returned to the kitchen where Vanessa was waiting. "I'm sorry about that."

Vanessa wrapped her arms around Grace in a hug. "You have nothing to apologize for. He was way out of line."

"I swear I didn't do it," Grace said, tears threatening to flow. Now that the confrontation was over and her anger had subsided, her emotions were catching up.

"No one who knows you would believe you'd do something like that," Vanessa reassured her. "Which is too bad for him, because the real culprit might not be as sweet as you are."

Grace looked at Vanessa in horror. "Do you think he's in danger?"

"I don't know," Vanessa said, shaking her head. "It seemed harmless enough, but who does something like that?"

"Someone who wants to teach him a lesson, I guess," Grace mused.

Vanessa grabbed her purse and took Grace's hand. "Let's forget about this and go shopping, okay? We have a hotel to decorate, and I, for one, am looking forward to it!"

"I hope you still feel that way once you see how big a job it is," Grace said, a smile lighting her face despite her tears.

"Nah," Vanessa waved her hand. "We'll just get the guys to do the heavy lifting."

Grace laughed. "If we feed them, they will come."

"You got that right!"

-Fifteen-

Grace quickly exited the diner shortly after the seven o'clock meeting. Without Lyda there to part the crowd, it had been difficult to slip out without getting caught up, but she'd managed. Derek, to her immense delight, had not fared as well. As soon as he'd tried to leave, as if on cue, all of the single and not-so-single women descended on him. He probably loved the attention, but it still made her smile to know he'd be stuck there for another twenty to thirty minutes.

Once she reached her car, she noticed a police vehicle parked next to it and groaned aloud when Officer Smith emerged.

"Aw, c'mon, Grace, I thought we were past all this," Officer Smith said.

"I'd like to think so, too, but we never seem to meet on good terms, do we?"

Officer Smith shook his head. "No, I guess not, and I'm afraid today won't be any different."

"Let me guess, you're here because of Derek and that card he received yesterday?" she asked dryly. He nodded, and she shook her head in frustration. "This is why we don't get along. Last Easter, you allowed my family to be terrorized for weeks by Dot and her cronies all because you couldn't arrest people on—and I quote—'gossip and rumors,' yet here you are badgering me over less than that."

"He's the mayor," Officer Smith said sheepishly.

"So the mayor gets special treatment the rest of us 'ordinary citizens' don't?"

Derek appeared beside Grace, as if materializing out of thin air. "Yes, Grace, that's exactly right." A wide grin spread across his face as he stared at her, arms crossed defiantly.

"Mayor Allen would never, ever act like this," Grace spat. "You should be ashamed of yourself, using your position to harass a resident."

"Wait a minute," Derek said, raising his hands. His grin quickly faded into a look of concern. "I'm not doing anything of the sort." He looked to Officer Smith for support. "Tell her that's not what I'm doing."

Officer Smith considered both of them for a moment. "I have no idea what's going on here, but Miss Parker has denied your accusations. I'm afraid there's nothing more to be done at this time." He turned to Derek. "Please notify us immediately if you receive any more threats."

"Am I free to go?" Grace asked. She couldn't believe those words had come out of her mouth. Since when had she been associated with crime? She was the person in charge of turning their town into Santa's Village—she hosted fundraisers and helped reunite estranged families, for Pete's sake. But maybe that was the perfect cover. Or perhaps it was a reminder that bad things happened to good people.

"Yes, ma'am," Officer Smith said with a nod. "Would you like an escort home?"

Derek threw his hands up in frustration. "Why are you asking her that? I'm the one who received the threatening card, not her. You should be offering me an escort!"

"I'll be fine, thank you," Grace replied, surprising herself with how gracious she sounded. Maybe she had been too hard on him—he was only trying to do his job, and with Derek breathing down his neck, that was probably not easy.

Grace climbed into her car and waited patiently for Derek to move. The last thing she needed was for him to claim she'd tried to run him over. With nothing else to do, she checked her email on her phone. To her surprise, she had a message from Rebekah:

Hey Grace,

A large family has booked the winery for a New Year's Eve anniversary party. They're looking for local accommodations and we naturally thought of the B&B—well, more specifically, the hotel. I've attached the information and will check in with you about it later today.

–Rebekah

Grace opened the attachment and cringed: fifty-four people needed rooms. She had never hosted that many guests in her life; not even close. Worse, they expected to start check-ins the day after Christmas, which meant she would have to move the New Year's guests in at the same time she moved the Christmas guests out. Could she really manage that? Did she want to try?

When she looked up, both Derek and Officer Smith were gone, so she started the car and slowly pulled out of the parking lot. So far, the hotel had felt more like a curse than a blessing—but groups this large could change that. On the other hand, this was Cole's off-season, the one time of year she could spend a decent amount of time with him. Would the money be worth that sacrifice? If it were just her, the answer would obviously be no. But it wasn't just her, was it?

With a sigh, she pulled into her driveway and studied her house. The lights were hung, and the new nutcrackers flanked the front door, but to her, it still looked drab. She'd have to do something about that. Right after she talked to Rebekah.

***

Grace walked into the kitchen and found Grant, Molly, and Rebekah waiting for her. While it was normal for them to be there at this time, Grace couldn't help but feel she was walking into an ambush.

"I take it you've told them?" Grace asked Rebekah.

Rebekah nodded, looking apologetic. "If you mean the New Year's event, yes. I wasn't trying to go behind your back; it's just that time is of the essence, and I needed an answer, like, yesterday."

It would have been nice to make a decision without Molly and Grant there to remind her of their financial situation, but if Grace was going to be a business owner, she supposed she had to care about the bottom line. "All right, then, lay it on us," Grace said.

As she listened to Rebekah, Grace pulled eggs and bacon from the fridge and started breakfast. She had a feeling in the pit of her stomach that she'd be roped into this, so the conversation was a mere formality at this point.

"So, two siblings are throwing a large fiftieth-wedding-anniversary party for their parents," Rebekah explained. "From what I understand, the parents married at midnight on New Year's Eve fifty years ago, so the party will start around nine and run until about two at the latest."

"Out of curiosity, why did they wait until the last minute to plan?" Grace asked. "They've known this anniversary was coming for years."

Rebekah shrugged. "I've heard a rumor they booked another venue and it fell through, but who knows. Regardless, they know they're cutting it close and are willing to pay a pretty penny for last-minute accommodations."

Grace looked at Molly and Grant. "And you two think this is a good idea?"

Grant put his arm around Molly's shoulders and squeezed her close. "It would be a great opportunity," he said.

Molly exchanged a glance with Grant, then turned to Grace. "While I agree it's a great opportunity, since the bulk of the work will fall to you, my chief concern is whether you can handle it."

The old Grace from a year ago would have taken offense at that; the new Grace was wondering the same thing. "Are you asking if I'm capable?" she pressed, defensively.

"No, of course not," Molly reassured her. "I'm asking if it's feasible. Rebekah showed me the guest list, and there are over fifty people on it. That's a lot of meals to cook, rooms to clean, and people to entertain. Not to mention they'll start arriving just as your other guests are departing. You won't have time to transition between the two."

"I need to talk to Jilly and see if she's available," Grace replied. "Without her, there simply won't be enough hands. With her, maybe we can pull this off."

"How soon can you get back to me?" Rebekah asked.

Apparently time really was of the essence. Grace sighed and pulled out her phone. "I'll text her now and see if she can talk."

"Thanks, Grace. I know this is pushing it, but if you can get an answer to me by lunch, I'd really appreciate it," Rebekah said, her hands clasped in a pleading gesture.

"This is really important to you, isn't it?" Grace asked.

Rebekah nodded. "This is the kind of client that can put my business on the map. I love living here, but Winterwood simply doesn't have enough people to sustain an event-planning company. If I'm going to succeed, I need to show people we're worth making the trip for, you know?"

Boy, did she know. "I'll get back to you by lunchtime," Grace promised. Her phone dinged and she saw Jilly would be available after breakfast. So Grace made plans to meet her, then finished serving everyone.

Once she was alone again, she took stock of her remaining Christmas decorations. A portion would need to go to the hotel, but that left her with some adorable inflatables she just knew her guests would love. While she waited for Jilly, she carried the boxes outside and set to work. She'd just gotten Santa and his reindeer set up when a voice called out behind her.

"Think we'll have a white Christmas?"

Grace jumped, the box flying from her hands. She spun around, only to come face-to-face with Jilly.

"Sorry, I didn't mean to scare you," Jilly said with a laugh. She bent down, retrieved the box, and handed it to Grace. "What's up?"

"First off, how have you been?" Grace asked as she accepted the box. "I feel like I haven't seen you in forever."

Jilly nodded, a sad look crossing her face. "Things have been difficult, but we're managing."

"Anything I can do to help?"

"I always need work," Jilly blurted. Her cheeks turned bright red as she looked down. "Sorry, I shouldn't have said that."

Grace studied the woman. She'd only known Jilly a couple of months, but in that time had come to consider her a good friend. It was clear she was hurting, but Grace didn't know what to do about that. Work, however, was a different matter. "Actually, that's why I texted you," Grace explained. "I have a lot of work if you're interested."

"Absolutely!" Jilly replied immediately.

"Don't you want to know what it is?" Grace asked with a laugh.

Jilly shook her head. "It doesn't matter. I'm serious, Grace, I'll do whatever you need."

There was a hint of desperation in her voice, and Grace couldn't help but wonder what happened to make Jilly feel that way. Should she ask? Or would that be overstepping? Since she wasn't sure, she decided to make herself available in case Jilly ever wanted to talk.

"In that case, I have guests arriving in eight days that I need to prepare for here, and then over fifty guests arriving at the hotel the day after Christmas. We still need to finish decorating, plan the menu, do the shopping, and clean the rooms. Once they've arrived, we'll need to cook, freshen the rooms, and help facilitate the planned activities. I'll graciously accept whatever help you can give."

"Just tell me what to do, and I'll do it," Jilly said.

Grace nodded. "Okay, for now, do you want to help me finish setting up my little village? I still have Santa's workshop and a couple of snowmen to inflate. Then, if you have time, I need to go to the hotel and hang decorations there." She'd planned to do that yesterday, but the trip had tired Vanessa out, and if Grace was honest, she hadn't been feeling it, either. So she'd decided to leave that bit of fun for future Grace, and now here she was.

"Sounds good to me," Jilly replied.

It was obvious Jilly was trying to keep a positive attitude, but Grace wasn't entirely convinced. Still, it wasn't her place to grill Jilly. All she could do was hope that, over time,

Jilly would either confide in her or that the situation would resolve itself.

-Fourteen-

For the first time in maybe forever, Grace slept through her alarm. It was also possible she'd been so tired the night before she'd forgotten to set it. Regardless, by the time she finally woke, it was well past time for the seven o'clock meeting—a fact she was sure Derek would use against her at every opportunity.

Since there was nothing she could do about it now, she decided to get dressed and go downstairs. It was also past time for breakfast, so it would be interesting to see if anyone had filled in for her.

Once downstairs, she was relieved to find that Molly had indeed stepped in and made breakfast for everyone. There was even a plate for Grace warming in the oven.

"You look like death warmed over," Molly said as she handed Grace the plate.

Grace gratefully accepted it and sat down at the breakfast bar to eat. "I feel like it, too," she mumbled. She had no idea why. Yesterday had been a good day: after she and Jilly finished setting up the inflatables here, they'd gone to the hotel, and with a little help—okay, with a lot of help—hung the decorations there, too. Once that was done, they'd ordered poinsettia centerpieces from Linda at Rustic Petals and Posies for both the B&B and the hotel. All in all, it had been very productive.

Molly watched Grace eat, a look of concern on her face. "I think we may have asked too much of you," she said quietly.

That was possible—probable, really—but how could Grace have said no? Jilly and Rebekah were counting on her. When Grace had needed help last year, countless people had stepped up. How could she turn her back when it was time to pay it forward? Simply put, she couldn't.

"I'll be all right," Grace said, forcing a smile. "It's only a few weeks out of my life, then I'll be able to take a break."

"No, then you'll be getting married," Molly reminded her.

Grace groaned. "Can't I just elope?" she whined.

Molly bumped Grace's shoulder. "Ordinarily, I'd say yes, but Granny and Gladys have been working non-stop on your wedding dress. It would crush them if they didn't get to see you wear it."

Well, she couldn't let that happen. "Okay, fine. After the wedding, I will take a much-needed break, unless you're going to tell me I have to host another Experience afterward?"

"Nope," Molly replied. "I'll give you the entire month of February off if you want it. I can't guarantee anything past that, though."

"Fair enough," Grace said. She checked her watch, winced, and added, "I guess we need to get to work."

They stood, Grace going one way and Molly the other.

"I am here for you," Molly called from the doorway. "I know I've been preoccupied with work and the baby, but I'm here if you need me."

Grace smiled, this time genuinely. "Thanks, Molly. I appreciate the reminder."

"Anytime," Molly said, waving lightly as she continued to the door and closed it gently behind her.

***

Since she'd missed the morning meeting, Grace decided to go downtown to see how things were progressing. Yesterday, she'd discovered that most Main Street businesses had already finished decorating their storefronts—save one or two—but the town itself hadn't hung any decorations yet. Given how close they were to Christmas Eve, she was concerned.

Next year, she decided, they would start decorating right after Thanksgiving, just like every other town. It was silly they hadn't done that this year, but to be fair, she hadn't planned on hosting a Christmas Experience. Still, was that really the only reason to decorate? Shouldn't Winterwood decorate regardless of one person's plans? Grace thought so. But maybe no one else had stepped up.

The closer she got to town hall, the worse she felt. Don't look, she told herself. If you don't see it, you don't have to stop. Unfortunately, she saw it anyway: a group of people huddled on the front lawn while an irate Derek and a tearful Katie argued among them. Grace really should keep going. If she tried to intervene, it would only make things worse.

I'm not stopping, she told herself as she pulled over in front of the building. Now that she'd stopped, there was only one thing she could do: she got out of the car and approached Derek and Katie.

"What's wrong?" Grace asked Katie. Now that she was closer, she could see Katie had been crying, and Grace was immediately concerned.

"Oh great, it's you," Derek said. "Too busy to attend this morning's meeting, but not too busy to interfere, I see."

Grace ignored him and focused on Katie. "Is there something I can do to help?"

Katie shook her head. "We went downstairs to get the decorations and discovered the basement had flooded during last week's storm. Some survived, but the majority are either ruined or covered in mold."

That was unexpected, but not surprising, Grace remembered her own decorations being destroyed. "I take it the 'mayor' won't allow replacements?" she asked, turning to Derek.

But Derek held up a hand before she could continue. "You know the rules, Grace. I cannot authorize anyone to spend large sums of money without the council's approval."

"So call a council meeting," Grace said sarcastically.

Derek crossed his arms. "I don't have everyone's phone numbers. Besides, I'm busy."

"Fine," Grace said, adopting his stance. "I'll call the meeting. And if you're too busy to attend, Katie can take your place."

"Oh, you'd love that, wouldn't you?" he spat. "Fine, call your little meeting, but I intend to oppose you."

"So what else is new?" Grace quipped. Then she turned back to Katie. "I'll contact the others and arrange a time; okay?"

Katie wiped her eyes and nodded. "Thanks, Grace."

"You're welcome." Grace looked at Derek. "You should be ashamed of yourself for making her cry."

Before he could respond, she marched back to her car and drove to Bea's Bakery. If anyone could help fix this, it was Bea—and the sooner, the better.

***

Getting everyone together during business hours wasn't easy, but they managed to schedule a two-o'clock meeting. This time, Grace arrived early, determined not to let Derek pull any tricks. However, she needn't have worried, he was nearly fifteen minutes late. While she would have preferred to start without him, she didn't want to appear petty.

When he finally rushed in, he launched right into the meeting.

"Sorry I'm late," he said, out of breath. "A meeting with a client ran longer than expected." He shot Grace a dirty look, then addressed the council. "I'll make this quick: the town's decorations are ruined, so we can't use them.

While that will disappoint some, it's simply not fiscally responsible to replace them now."

"Can you explain why?" Junior asked skeptically.

Derek took a breath. "Of course. Simply put, the decorations are expensive and can only be ordered through catalogs. If—and it's a very big if—you could even get them this close to Christmas, rush shipping would cost a fortune."

Junior exchanged glances with his wife, Bea, then looked at Grace. "I'm sorry, darlin', but I have to agree with Derek. The town still looks festive. I'm sure no one will even notice they're gone."

"But what about the park decorations?" Grace asked. "Or the ones for the tree-lighting ceremony? People will notice those are missing."

Derek shrugged. "You'll just have to cancel the tree ceremony and replace it with something else."

Grace's heart sank. She looked around helplessly. "Does everyone agree?" she asked, though she already knew the answer.

Addie reached over and patted her hand. "It will be okay," she said.

Derek smiled. "Let's vote. All those in favor, say 'aye.'" No one raised a hand or said anything. "All opposed?" Every hand in the room except Grace's rose.

Grace didn't vote—why would she, when it was obvious they'd turned against her? First her wedding plans had been derailed; now her Christmas Experience was collapsing, too.

With nothing left to discuss, Derek adjourned the meeting. Grace couldn't stand his smug look, so she hurried out, only to have Derek grab her arm before she reached the door.

"I told you I was coming for you," he sneered.

"Congratulations, you really are Scrooge," she shot back. "What do you have against Christmas? Did Santa leave coal in your stocking when you were a wee lad?"

Derek snorted. "You think you know everything. I bet you woke up to piles of presents every Christmas morning."

Grace tried to remember life before moving in with Granny, but those memories were hazy. "I suppose that could have happened when I was very young, before my parents died. After that, Granny and I were too poor: I got socks, underwear, and pajamas. When she could afford it, my stocking held peanuts and a couple of dollar-store toys."

"You're just saying that to make me feel guilty," he stammered.

"No, I'm not. I've learned that Scrooge doesn't feel guilty about anything, remember?"

He took a step closer, eyes narrowing. "You keep calling me Scrooge," he accused. "I know it was you who sent that card."

"That's two things you're wrong about," she said. "Now, if you'll excuse me, I need to figure out how to replace an entire tree-lighting ceremony."

Grace turned on her heel and left. She'd have slammed the double-swinging door if she could. Once safely in her car, she rested her forehead on the steering wheel. What was she supposed to do now? Molly had made promises to her guests—guests who were paying a lot of money to come here for a traditional Christmas Experience.

The question wasn't whether she could replace the ceremony, but whether she could replace it with something better. And that was a question she honestly couldn't answer.

-Thirteen-

Since Grace had missed the meeting the day before, she made sure she arrived not only on time but early for this morning's meeting. When it was time to start, she walked to the front of the room, surprised to see the crowd had grown. As usual, Derek sat at a table in front of her, playing on his phone.

"Good morning, everyone," she greeted, forcing a huge smile. She absolutely did not feel like smiling, but the people who'd been working so hard deserved a show of appreciation. She'd never make it in politics, but she would do her best for her beloved town.

Before she could say "Does anyone have questions?" a woman seated at a table in the middle of the room raised her hand. When Grace nodded at her, the woman stood and addressed her.

"There's a rumor going around that the town's decorations have been destroyed. Is that true?" the woman asked.

Grace nodded, eyes downcast. "I'm afraid it is. That last storm flooded the basement at town hall, and most of the decorations were ruined."

"Is there a plan to replace them?" the woman asked.

Don't look at him, don't look at him, Grace told herself. "I'm afraid that won't be possible at this time," she stated as neutrally as she could.

The woman—clearly disappointed—sat down.

"What does that mean?" called out another voice from the back.

Grace looked around and saw Mandy, Molly's aunt, waving. "It means we won't be able to hang the lights on Main Street, and there will be no tree-lighting ceremony at the end of the parade," Grace explained. She glanced at Derek, who watched her intently—probably waiting for her to throw him under the bus. She refused. She would not undermine Mayor Allen or the town council just to punish Derek, something he'd know if he weren't so busy assuming the worst of everyone.

"Huh," Mandy said as she processed the news. "I have some extra lights, and I'm sure other people have decorations they're not using. What if we donate them?"

"Oh, I have a ton that's been collecting dust in my attic for years," said an older woman. "I'd love to see them put to use."

Tears stung Grace's eyes as she watched her community once again come together to solve a problem. "That would be amazing," she said once she found her voice. "This would make the tree truly special, a real community tree."

"I'll lead a committee to help collect the donations," Addie called from behind the counter. "And everyone is welcome to help decorate the tree."

"Thank you, Addie, that would be great!" Grace exclaimed.

With renewed excitement, Grace faced the crowd. "Thank you all so much. When I arrived this morning, I felt the crushing weight of disappointment in my chest, but now, thanks to all of you, that weight is gone and in its place is hope. This is the true meaning of Christmas: friends and family coming together to spread love and joy." She looked at Derek, hoping her words had affected him; he only rolled his eyes. "Any other questions or concerns?" When no one spoke up, Grace ended the meeting.

It took some time to work through the crowd as many attendees wanted to talk to her. She'd just reached her car when a hand clasped her shoulder, stopping her in her tracks.

"That was quite the Hallmark moment back there," Derek said sarcastically.

"I'd really like to know what happened to you to turn you into such a cold, bitter man," Grace replied. "I've met some hardhearted people, but I think you might be the worst—maybe second-worst," she hedged. "There was a woman who tried to ruin Easter for little kids last year."

"I like this woman already," Derek deadpanned.

Grace nodded. "I thought you would say that. Well, sorry your plans were thwarted. I guess you'll just have to try harder to ruin Christmas."

"I always did love a good challenge," Derek replied.

"So do I," Grace said, a grin spreading across her face. "Since every villain needs a hero, I'm going to make it my mission to transform you from Scrooge into a full-blown Christmas convert."

"Want to place a bet on that?"

Grace shook her head. "No, I'm pretty sure you'll lose no matter what."

Derek glared at her, then shook his head. "You're the most infuriating person I've ever met."

"Again," Grace shrugged, "you're either number one or number two for me, too. So I guess we're even."

"Whatever," he muttered, turning on his heel and stomping off toward his car.

She watched him go, her anger and frustration toward him shifting to sadness and pity. Somehow, she would find a way to get through to him. She just hoped she could do so before he ruined Christmas for good.

***

Grace had just pulled into her driveway when her phone dinged. She grabbed it and saw a text from Cole:

Hey babe, can you come out to the farm?

She was about to reply when the date at the top of the screen caught her eye—today was supposed to have been their wedding day. As she sat in her driveway, trying to process that, she realized how foolish she'd been to rush something so important. Their wedding should be more than an afterthought:

I'll be there as soon as breakfast is over.

She was about to get out of the car when three little dots appeared, and a new reply from Cole showed up:

Rebekah will handle breakfast. Please come now.

Grace read and reread the message, looking for hidden meaning. Was something wrong? Was he hurt? Were the animals okay? In all the time they'd been together, he'd never once asked her to drop everything and come over.

Her hands shook as she typed:

Be right there.

She then drove as fast as she dared to the farm. Thankfully, it was only about a five-minute drive. If it had taken any longer, she would have had time to work herself into a serious anxiety attack.

When she arrived, she hurried inside and did a quick headcount. Ruby and Max were in their usual spots in front of the fireplace, wagging their tails as soon as they saw her. Piper was curled up in a ball on the couch, which meant she was unharmed. That left Cole. Oh gosh, was he hurt?

"Cole?" she called, her voice trembling with worry.

"Just a minute," he shouted from somewhere deeper in the house.

Grace's brow furrowed. When he appeared a few minutes later, hands full of boxes, she did a once-over and sighed with relief—he was okay.

Cole set the boxes on the dining room table, then pulled Grace into his arms. "Sorry about that. I didn't expect you to get here so fast." He kissed her several times, then eagerly guided her to the table.

"Hold on a second," Grace said, pulling back to look at him. "What's going on? I rushed over because I was scared something awful had happened, yet everyone seems fine."

"Oh, wow," Cole said, pulling her into a hug. "I'm sorry, what did I say to make you think something was wrong?"

She breathed in his familiar scent as she rested her cheek against his chest. If there was one person she couldn't live without, it was him. "I guess you didn't say anything, it's just that you've never summoned me like that before, so I assumed something terrible had happened."

Cole pulled back and gazed deep into her eyes, one hand cupping her cheek. "How about this: if anything ever happens in the future, I promise I'll call you, okay?"

"No texts?" she asked.

"Never," he replied, grinning. "Now, are you ready for my surprise?"

A tiny part of her wanted to point out that he could have texted her about the surprise, but her curiosity overrode that. "Yes!" she said enthusiastically. The last time he had surprised her, he'd proposed, so now she was extra curious.

Cole chuckled, then turned to the boxes. "Sorry about all the dust, these boxes have been in the attic for at least a decade." He motioned for her to come closer. "Please look inside?"

Grace cautiously lifted the lid of the first box and gasped. "Oh my gosh, these are beautiful," she exclaimed, pulling out a delicate glass ornament. She held it to the light, mesmerized by its sparkle, then pressed it to her chest. "Please tell me you aren't donating these to the town. While that would be lovely, they're too precious for an outdoor tree."

"What?" he asked, confused. "No, actually, these belonged to my mother. She spent years collecting them and considered them her prized possessions."

"I can see why," Grace said as she carefully lifted more bulbs. She admired each one in the sunlight, imagining what they would look like on their tree. "Thank you for sharing something so special to you and your mom."

Cole turned her to face the living room, where a large, unlit Christmas tree stood by the sliding doors. "I take it you missed that?" he asked.

When she gasped in surprise, he chuckled and wrapped his arms around her, kissing her cheek. "You must have been really upset."

Grace nodded, resting the back of her head against his chest. "Today was supposed to be our wedding day," she sighed. "But I guess this means we'll have two firsts: our first Christmas as a couple, and next year our first Christmas as husband and wife."

He kissed her cheek again and rested his chin on top of her head. "That sounds wonderful."

Grace turned and wrapped her arms around his neck. "I think you're wonderful. Thank you for doing this for me. It feels like the day is still special, even if we had to postpone the wedding."

His face grew serious. "Are you sure you want to use my mom's ornaments? We can always buy new ones..."

"Are you kidding?" Grace smiled, lifting one of the glass bulbs. "After losing all of my family's decorations in the storm, I'm honored to have your mom's. Honey, your family is as important as mine, and I'm happy to honor them. Besides, we're going to have the most beautiful tree in Winterwood—can't argue with that!"

"I love you," he said, gazing into her eyes.

"I love you, too, now and forever." She stood on her tiptoes to kiss him, then set the ornament aside and picked up the TV remote. "There's only one thing that will make this better."

Cole leaned against the wall, arms crossed. "And what's that?"

"Christmas music!" Grace exclaimed, switching to a holiday station.

***

Halfway through their decorating extravaganza, Grace paused to make hot chocolate with marshmallows. When they finished, they curled up on the couch and stared at their handiwork.

"You're going to have a tough time keeping Piper out of the tree," Grace said as Piper batted at an ornament hanging low on a bottom branch.

"We've already given her a couple of stern talks," Cole chuckled.

"If she becomes too big a pest, I can take her back with me," Grace said absentmindedly. She couldn't bear the thought of leaving the farm. At some point, it had begun to feel more like home than her own home did.

Cole kissed the top of her head. "I would like to believe I can handle a cat," he teased. "If not, I may have to consider a new line of work!"

Grace tried to formulate a witty response but decided she'd rather kiss him instead. Moments alone like these were rare. No sense wasting them on banter.

-Twelve-

The daily meeting had been quick that morning, and Grace was hopeful she was nearing the time when they would no longer be necessary. Once her guests arrived, she'd be needed at the B&B to fulfill the 'breakfast' part of bed and breakfast. If only Derek could be counted on to fill in if needed. Grace quickly dismissed the thought—if he didn't want to be a team player, so be it.

She had just set the last plate of eggs on the table when the group began filing in and taking their seats. "Good morning," Grace called out as she went back for the pot of coffee.

"Good morning," Molly, Grant, Emilio, Granny, and Gladys replied in unison.

After she poured coffee for everyone, Grace took her seat—just in time to see Molly slide a piece of paper across the table to her. "What's this?" Grace asked, picking it up and glancing at the list of names.

"That," Molly said, pointing to the paper with her fork, "is your guest list."

Grace looked at the paper with renewed interest. "Let's see," she said, reading through the names a second time.

"Carl and his sister Katherine are coming," she announced excitedly. Then she turned to Granny. "I can't wait to see them again!"

"Me neither," Granny replied, reaching across the table to squeeze Grace's hand. "How long has it been since we saw Carl?"

"Not since March," Grace reminded her.

Granny nodded. "Oh yes, that's right. He stopped by on his way to New Orleans when he was moving there to be closer to his family. How is his brother doing?"

"I'm afraid Edward passed away before Thanksgiving," Grace said quietly. Poor Carl, she thought. Last year he'd lost his wife around this time, and now he'd lost his brother, too. She hated that her dear friend would once again spend the holidays mourning, and she was determined to make this year just as special as last.

"I'm sorry to hear that," Granny said thoughtfully, sitting silently for a moment as if recalling her own losses.

As Grace watched Granny, an idea popped into her head: she'd have to call Katherine later and ask for a small favor before they left Louisiana.

While Grace and Granny pondered, the room grew quiet, so Grace figured she'd better liven things up a bit. "Back to the list," she said cheerfully. "It looks like there's a family of five coming, two teenagers and a baby?" she asked Molly, eyebrows raised.

Molly nodded. "I think it was a 'surprise' baby," she said with a laugh. "Parents are Teddy and Hannah, then the twins: Leo and Leora, who are fourteen, and baby Lexi."

"That's a lot of people in one room, but I think we can make it work," Grace replied. She visualized the bedrooms and tried to fit all the beds Tetris-style. If worse came to worst, she could give up her own room and stay at Cole's. What a hardship!

"Then there's Arnie, Louisa, and their baby Rosalyn," Molly added, again pointing at the paper with her fork.

Grace glanced between Molly and the list. "I'm sensing a bit of a theme," she teased.

Grant—who had been reading the newspaper—looked up. "You know Eliza's a little young for play dates?" he asked Molly.

"I know," Molly said sheepishly. "I just thought it would be fun to have other moms around to share some 'firsts,' you know?"

"Oh, I see," Grant nodded. "The play dates are for you."

Rebekah poured a second cup of coffee as she watched the exchange. "Am I missing something?"

"I think Molly feels a little isolated since she's the only one in our group with a baby," Grace explained.

"Oh, well I can't help you there," Rebekah shrugged. "I'm more of the 'fun aunt' type, if you know what I mean."

Grace sensed an undercurrent of bitterness in Rebekah's words and vowed to talk to her about it later. For now, she steered the conversation back to safer waters. "It looks like we have one more couple?" she asked Molly.

Molly winced as she prepared to break the news. "Yes, Ross and Megan."

"And what's so special about them?" Grace asked. She'd noticed Molly's hesitant look and knew there was more to the story.

"They're newlyweds, so this is their first Christmas as husband and wife," Molly explained.

That explained it. Grace felt a momentary pang of jealousy, but it disappeared as quickly as it came. Yes, she would have loved to celebrate her first Christmas as Cole's wife this year, but she'd made peace with that and could be happy for this couple. She made a mental note to add a bottle of champagne to Ross and Megan's welcome basket.

"Is there anything else I should know?" Grace asked. They tried to gather as much information about their guests as possible, without being intrusive. Since they offered an 'experience' and not just a place to sleep, it was important to Grace to create a home-away-from-home atmosphere.

"Well, actually," Molly said hesitantly, "there is one more thing."

"Why do I get the feeling I'm not going to like this?" Grace groaned.

Molly gave her a sympathetic look. "One of the twins—Leo or Leora—has a gluten allergy. So he or she needs all their food to be gluten-free. And, according to Hannah, that includes eliminating any possibility of cross-contamination."

Grace stared at Molly, trying to process this new complication. "And you agreed to this?" she asked skeptically. What did she know about cooking gluten-free?

Or whatever cross-contamination meant? While she'd admit her cooking skills had improved since last Christmas, she was by no means a professional.

"They've agreed to pay extra," Molly said, as if that solved everything.

"I can't believe this," Grace said, shaking her head. "There's already so much to do, and now I'm expected to learn an entirely new way of cooking in about..." She checked her watch. "...five days?"

Molly shrugged. "I'm sorry; it didn't seem like a big deal at the time."

"It never seems like a big deal when you're not the one doing it," Grace snapped. She took a deep, calming breath, then stood and began clearing plates. "I guess I'll figure it out," she muttered.

Rebekah stood and began helping. "We could always cancel," she proposed. "Tell them we're sorry, but we can't accommodate their needs at this time."

Grace stopped at the sink and turned to face her friend. "While I agree that's a good idea, I can't do that to them right before the biggest holiday of the year. I'll just have to figure out a way to make it work." She resumed rinsing plates. "Somehow," she muttered.

As she finished tidying the kitchen, an idea popped into her head. There was one person who might be able to help; all she had to do was pay her a visit.

***

Little bells jingled as Grace opened the door to Bea's Bakery, the scent of cinnamon and ginger wafting through the air. Her mouth watered at the sight of donuts, cookies, and cakes displayed in the glass case down the middle of the room. Even though she'd just had breakfast, she decided to treat herself to one of those delectable goodies—after all, with everything going on, she deserved a little pick-me-up.

"Hey, Jenny," Grace said to Bea's long-time assistant. "I'll take one of those gingerbread men, please."

"Coming right up," Jenny replied, though her normally cheerful face looked somewhat sour.

Grace was about to ask if everything was okay when Bea emerged from the kitchen area.

"Oh, hello, Grace," Bea said, smiling when she saw her friend. "I thought I heard your voice!"

"You're just the person I wanted to see," Grace replied warmly. "Do you have a few minutes to talk?"

Bea glanced at her watch, then nodded. "Why don't you grab a seat while I get us some coffee?"

Since Grace was currently Bea's only customer, she chose the bistro-style table farthest from the door. Moments later, Bea returned with two cups of coffee and a plate of fresh-from-the-oven cinnamon rolls.

"So, are you here to discuss your cake?" Bea asked, pulling a notepad and pencil from her apron pocket and laying them on the table.

"Cake?" Grace replied, momentarily confused. "Oh, no," she said, shaking her head once she realized Bea meant the wedding cake. "I'm actually here to ask for advice."

Bea looked puzzled. "Okay, what about?"

Grace explained her gluten-free dilemma, then leaned back in her chair, waiting for Bea's response. The cinnamon rolls smelled too good to ignore, so Grace grabbed one and devoured it while she waited to hear Bea's thoughts.

Bea let out a low whistle. "That's quite the problem," she finally said. "It's not just a matter of providing gluten-free options, you also have to ensure there's no cross-contamination." She shook her head. "Honestly, if it were me, I'd simplify things by making all the food gluten-free."

"But I've always heard gluten-free isn't very good," Grace protested, crinkling her nose at the thought of serving inedible food. She grabbed another cinnamon roll despite her stomach's protestations that she'd already eaten enough.

"It will definitely be different, but there are plenty of good recipes out there. And a lot of meat and vegetable dishes are naturally gluten-free. You'll just have to get creative."

Great, because she had all the time in the world to "get creative." But what choice did she have? It wasn't the child's fault he had allergies; he shouldn't be punished for something he couldn't control. Grace sighed and set the cinnamon roll back on the plate. Then, a thought occurred to her and she leaned forward.

"What are you going to do with the bakery?" she asked in a low voice so Jenny—still working behind the counter—couldn't hear. "Is Jenny going to take over?"

Bea shook her head and leaned in. "I thought about it," she whispered. "But I don't think it makes sense. Jenny is a great assistant, but she lacks the skill and motivation to run this place on her own. Why, are you interested in the bakery?"

"Heavens, no," Grace replied. "I was just wondering what's going to happen here. You've been such a staple in our community for so long it feels depressing to think this place might close."

"It depresses me, too," Bea said, reaching across the table to pat Grace's hand. "Change is hard, but I have faith everything will work out as it's supposed to, even if that means this place closes for good."

Grace tried to smile, though it came out more like a grimace. "What will you and Junior do? You're not going to retire to Florida or Arizona, are you?"

"No," Bea shook her head, a small smile appearing. "Junior and I talked about buying a travel trailer and traveling the country, but that would mean he'd have to give up the farm, and I don't think he's ready for that. In fact, he may never be ready. Once farming gets in your blood, it's hard to get it out."

An image of Cole at Junior's age flashed before Grace's eyes. She had to admit he was still handsome, but she wasn't sure she loved the idea of him farming until he died. That was a problem for future Grace, right now, she already had enough to juggle.

"Maybe now you'll have time to join the sewing club Granny and Gladys keep talking about," Grace said absentmindedly, thinking of all the future might hold.

Whatever happened, she hoped everyone would end up happy. At the end of the day, that was what mattered most, though she'd be lying if she said she wouldn't miss Bea's cinnamon rolls and gingerbread cookies.

"I might just do that," Bea laughed. "I wish I could be more help with your gluten-free issue, but that's a road I never wanted to travel. If you get desperate, though, give me a call and I'll see what I can do."

Grace stood and pushed her chair in. "Thanks, Bea. I'll keep that in mind." She gave her friend a hug, then waved goodbye to Jenny, who still looked unhappy. Now that Grace had a plan, it was full steam ahead. The countdown to her guests' arrival had begun, and the clock was ticking.

-Eleven-

G race was in the kitchen working on her third test batch of gluten-free dinner rolls when Molly popped her head in through the door.

"Are you still mad at me?" Molly asked, brows raised. Without waiting for a response, she entered the room and sat down at the breakfast bar. "What are you doing?"

"I wasn't mad at you until I tried making these stupid rolls," Grace replied. She picked one up from the first batch and banged it on the counter. "Do you hear that? I'm pretty sure this could be classified as a weapon. Or, if Major League Baseball teams ever run out of baseballs, they could use these as replacements."

Molly laughed. "I'm sure it's not that bad."

"Did you miss the part where I just banged this on the counter?" Grace asked, waving the roll. Her tone came out sharper than intended.

"No, I didn't miss it," Molly said, her expression sobering. "But I do have good news. Since this whole fiasco is my fault, I've decided to make it right by hiring an experienced chef to cook for the duration of our guests' stay."

Dollar signs flashed before Grace's eyes as she imagined how much it would cost to pay someone to come to Winterwood each day and cook three meals. Add in snacks and desserts, and it would cost a small fortune. Even if the expense didn't completely consume their profits, was it fair to expect her to take a pay cut over something she had zero say in?

"I can tell by the look on your face that you're not as excited as I thought you'd be," Molly said dryly.

Grace took a calming breath, then leaned her elbows on the counter. "Normally, I'd be ecstatic to have such a large amount of work taken off my plate, but Molly, hiring a chef is a huge expense. I already feel put out that I have to switch my entire menu to a gluten-free one. Being forced to pay someone else to do the cooking feels like an added punishment."

"Do I need to remind you that you did just that during your first Christmas Experience?" Molly shot back.

Grace sighed. "Yes, but I carefully factored the cost of those meals into the price of the Experience, and I ordered those meals from local restaurants. You're talking about hiring a private chef for a specialized menu, those are not the same thing."

"I suppose that's fair," Molly conceded. "Regardless, I'm not asking you to pay for this. Since this is my fault, I will cover the cost personally." She held up a hand before Grace could protest. "Not only that, the chef will be here any minute to go over plans with you, so it's literally too late for you to say no."

Grace's mouth opened and closed a few times as she tried to gather her thoughts. Just as she was about to speak, the doorbell rang, putting an end to their dispute.

"I'll get it," Molly said, hopping off her barstool and heading for the door.

Muffled voices came from the foyer as Grace watched with bated breath for the mystery chef to make an entrance. She didn't have to wait long for the man in question to reveal himself, as none other than Derek Morgan came stomping into the room with Molly hot on his heels.

"Well, this is certainly a surprise," Grace deadpanned. "I had no idea you were a personal chef in your spare time," she added to Derek.

He looked at her in confusion, brow furrowed, then shook his head and held up a white envelope. "Look, I know we got off on the wrong foot, and it was one hundred percent my fault, but can you please stop it with the cards? Please," he implored, thrusting the envelope toward Grace.

It was tempting to make a joke, but he seemed so distressed Grace didn't have the heart. Instead, she accepted the envelope and opened it to find a card bearing a ghost illustration and the words **Ghost of Christmas Present** scrawled above it. Inside were pictures that appeared to have been taken of Derek recently—some in an office, others presumably at his home. There was nothing scandalous about them, but Grace could see why having one's picture taken without consent would be unnerving.

"I'm really sorry someone is doing this to you," she said, handing back the envelope. "But it honestly isn't me."

Derek ran a hand through his hair and stared off into the distance. "No," he said, shaking his head vehemently. "It has to be you; there is literally no one else it could be."

"I'm sorry, Derek, but unless I'm doing this in my sleep, it isn't me."

"You're the only one who has a grudge against me," he argued. "I haven't lived here in almost twenty years; all my old friends have moved away. I have no family here, and none of my city associates would do something like this. So who does that leave if not you?"

Grace tried as hard as she could to come up with an alternative, but drew a blank. Granny and Gladys were the only ones who'd heard her make the Scrooge joke, but she couldn't imagine either of them stalking Derek and taking photos. How could she convince him otherwise?

"I really have no idea who it could be," Grace replied, "but if it makes you feel better, the ghosts didn't visit Scrooge out of malice or revenge. They did it to show him the error of his ways. So it's very likely the person doing this cares about you." She gave him a big smile to emphasize her point, but it only seemed to agitate him more.

"There's nothing wrong with my life," he spat. "Just because I don't fall all over myself in excitement every time the word 'Christmas' is uttered doesn't mean I need some sort of intervention. People are allowed to not like the holidays, okay?"

It wasn't clear whether he was trying to convince Grace or himself, but he seemed sincere enough that she felt it was only right to agree. "You're right, no one has to love Christmas. I can't promise you won't get another card, but I can promise it won't be from me."

The doorbell rang a second time, and Molly—who had been silently watching—excused herself to answer it. She returned a moment later with Jilly.

Derek gave Jilly a once-over, then muttered something inaudible under his breath. "Can we please just do our best to get along until Allen returns?" he implored.

"I would like nothing more," Grace replied.

He studied her, as if trying to gauge her sincerity, then nodded. "Good, that's all I ask. Now, if you'll excuse me, I have to get to work."

"I need to go, too," Molly chimed in. "I'll walk you out." She led Derek toward the door.

Grace watched them go, then turned to Jilly. "I wasn't expecting you until later. What's up?"

"Didn't Molly tell you? I'm your new chef—ta-da!" Jilly said, throwing her arms out and grinning exaggeratedly.

"You have experience cooking gluten-free food?" Grace asked skeptically. Jilly did seem a Jill-of-all-trades—no pun intended—but Grace couldn't shake the feeling something else was going on.

Jilly nodded, smile fading. "My sister has celiac disease, so I've had a fair bit of experience."

"What about all the other things you're supposed to help me with?" Grace asked. "Even if you take over the food, I'll still need help with cleaning, especially since we have to get the hotel ready."

"I don't see why I can't do both," Jilly replied. Her hands trembled slightly as she crossed her arms, hiding them from view.

Concern etched Grace's face. "What's really going on?" she asked gently.

Jilly looked away, then back at Grace, tears stinging her eyes. "You know how I took the kids to spend Thanksgiving with their father's parents?" When Grace nodded, she continued. "Well, they're having a really hard time dealing with their son's death. Not that I blame them, if I lost one of my kids, I'd be a wreck, too. It's just..." She trailed off, tears flowing in earnest.

Grace walked over to a side table and grabbed a box of tissues. She returned to Jilly and handed it to her. "It's just what?" she prodded.

"They spent most of our trip trying to convince me to let the kids move in with them," Jilly whispered.

"I'm sorry, I don't think I heard you right," Grace replied. "It sounded like you said they want the kids to live with them, but that can't be true."

Jilly nodded, blowing her nose. "At first, they tried to make it sound like they were doing me a favor, just while I get back on my feet, you know? But when that didn't work, they started criticizing my parenting. They said that since I don't have full-time work or a place of my own, I'm not fit to be a mom."

Grace gasped, hand flying to her mouth. "They can't mean that."

"I didn't want to believe it either," Jilly said, "but right before we left, they told me to think long and hard about their offer. When I told them the answer would be no, they said I'd be hearing from their lawyer."

Grief makes people do things they'd never do otherwise, but this went beyond that. "I'm so sorry, Jilly," Grace said softly. "Surely they wouldn't take you to court, and even if they did, no judge in his right mind would side with them."

"They have money," Jilly sighed. "And while I have some leftover from my husband's life insurance policy, it's not enough to fight them and support my kids."

"What can I do?" Grace asked. There had to be a way to help her friend, and if not, she would find one.

Jilly blew her nose again, then tossed the used tissues in the garbage. "What I really need is a job and a place to live. I have to get ahead of this so if it comes to it, I can show the court that I'm more than capable of providing for my kids."

Grace tried to do some quick math in her head to see if she could hire Jilly full-time. Unfortunately, the numbers just weren't there, at least not yet. However... "I think I might have a solution, but I need to talk to someone first. For now, are you sure you still want to be our chef?" Grace picked up a couple of her dinner rolls—hockey pucks, really—and began to juggle them. "I won't say I've got this covered, but I definitely do not have this covered." As if on cue, she dropped one, and it landed with a loud thud on the wooden floor.

A laugh escaped Jilly as she leaned over the counter to inspect the carnage. "I don't think rolls are supposed to sound like that," she teased.

"I don't think so either," Grace agreed, staring at the offending object. "Maybe I should preserve it for posterity's sake?"

"I was thinking more along the lines of hiding the evidence," Jilly deadpanned.

Grace looked at Jilly's face and burst out laughing. Jilly quickly followed suit.

"Thanks, Grace," Jilly said, wiping tears from her eyes. "I needed that laugh."

"You know what? I did, too," Grace admitted. "Why don't you get to work on the menu while I make a phone call? If things go the way I'm hoping, we might have something to celebrate!"

Jilly nodded, pulling a notebook from her purse. "I've already started, just tell me which choices you approve."

"Sounds good. Just give me one minute," Grace replied. She grabbed her phone, then stepped out onto the back deck to call Bea. Jenny might not be the ideal choice to take over the bakery, but Jilly most certainly was. All Grace needed to do now was convince Bea.

-Ten-

G race finished the morning dishes and decided to check on Granny. Even though they lived in the same house, there were times it felt like she barely saw her beloved grandmother. Those times tended to coincide with the weeks leading up to the arrival of a new batch of guests, and Grace always felt guilty despite the financial necessity of her playing innkeeper.

When she opened the door to Granny's room, Granny and Gladys immediately stuffed what looked like magazines under the bedcovers, all the while alternating between giggling and trying to hush the other one.

"Why do you two look like a couple of schoolgirls who just got caught reading a steamy romance novel?" Grace asked, her brow raised.

Granny did her best to appear innocent. "Why Grace, I have no idea what you're talking about," she said in mock indignation.

"Really, Grace," Gladys huffed. "Accusing a couple of sweet, innocent women of such things." She clucked her tongue as she shook her head.

Their attempts to chide her would have worked had they been able to keep the smiles off their faces.

"You two," Grace said, shaking her head as she laughed. "What are you really up to in here?"

"Nothing you need to be concerned about, dear," Granny replied. "Gladys and I are just passing the time, that's all."

Grace eyed them suspiciously but decided to let it go. The difference between now and a year ago was almost shocking; Grace shuddered at the memory of how close she'd come to losing her granny. No, she would support whatever it was they were scheming as long as it kept that rosy glow of health on her grandmother's cheeks.

Ding! Grace looked down at her phone and saw a text message from Lyda:

Call me ASAP!

"It appears there may be trouble downtown," Grace announced. "Do you two need anything before I go?"

Gladys shook her head. "I'm pretty sure we have everything we need, and if we don't, these old bones are capable of getting up and getting it!"

"Oh, Gladys," Grace said with a laugh. "You're only as old as you feel!"

"You remember that when you're my age," Gladys joked. "Seriously, go take care of business. We'll be fine here, and if we're not, you're only a phone call away."

Grace gave them both a hug, then walked back to the kitchen to call Lyda. When Lyda answered on the first ring, an uneasy feeling settled over Grace.

"I'm so glad you called, you'll never guess what the mayor just did!" Lyda's words came out in a barely distinguishable rush.

"I'm not sure I want to know," Grace groaned.

Lyda laughed. "No, you probably don't, but that doesn't change the fact you need to get down here and help sort through this mess."

Did she really have to do that? Yes, of course, the answer was yes. "Okay, I'll be right there. Where should I meet you?"

"At the mayor's office," Lyda replied. "And Grace, make sure you come prepared for war." Without waiting for a reply, Lyda hung up the phone.

Okay, that did not sound good. Grace stared at her phone for a moment before sighing and grabbing her purse. Whatever the problem, there is a solution, Grace muttered under her breath. Even if that solution is to bulldoze straight through all two hundred pounds of their infuriating, stubborn, Scrooge of a mayor.

***

Lyda was pacing outside town hall when Grace arrived, but that wasn't the first thing Grace noticed. No, the first thing she noticed was that all the decorations that had just been hung the day before were now gone.

"What happened?" Grace asked Lyda as she swept her arm to indicate the now bare building.

"You know who happened," Lyda replied. "And that's not all. He announced at the meeting this morning that he was officially closing the ice skating rink."

Grace's eyes went wide. "Why on earth did he do that?" Memories of her first time ice skating last year flooded her mind. The whole town, not to mention her guests, had seemed to love the experience, and she hated the thought of disappointing them this year.

"You'll have to ask him," Lyda told Grace. "He didn't give a reason at the meeting, and he was so quick to leave afterwards, no one got a chance to talk to him."

"Alright then, I guess it's time for a chat," Grace said as she stormed past Lyda and into the building. When Katie saw her, she immediately waved Grace and Lyda into Derek's office. "What happened to our truce?" Grace asked angrily as she burst through the door.

Derek looked up from his computer. "What do you mean?"

Grace rolled her eyes and scoffed. "What do you think I mean? First you take down all the decorations, then you cancel the ice-skating rink. Those are not the actions of someone who just yesterday was begging for my forgiveness."

"I hardly consider asking you to stop harassing me with those silly cards of yours to be 'begging for forgiveness,'" he said dryly. "Furthermore, those 'decorations' were a gaudy mismatch of dollar store rejects, so unless you're looking to win the tackiest Christmas display competition, they had to go."

The sound of cowboy boots clicking across the linoleum floor momentarily caught their attention. Three pairs of eyes simultaneously turned to stare at the door as they waited to see who the boots belonged to. When Cole appeared in the doorway, Grace rushed into his arms, forgetting all about the fight she was having with Derek.

"I can't believe this," Derek called out in frustration. "First you bring your granny to our meeting, now you bring your boyfriend. Can't you just once fight your own battles?"

Cole turned to Derek and gave him a hard look. "That's fiancé," he said coldly. "Grace doesn't need my help fighting her battles, but that doesn't mean I'm willing to stand by and allow people to attack her."

Derek raised his hands in front of him. "Now hold on there, cowboy, nobody's attacking anybody here. I was just pointing out we're all adults, and there's no need for all this extra drama."

"What exactly seems to be the problem?" Cole asked Derek. His arms were still wrapped around Grace as he continued to stare Derek straight in the eye.

"Um," Derek hesitated as he cleared his throat. "I was just informing your, uh, fiancée, that the decorations were not fit for display, so we had to take them down."

Cole looked at Grace. "Is it important to you that the town hall is decorated?"

Grace nodded. "It's the only building that doesn't have decorations," she explained. "My guests are expecting a winter wonderland. What kind of message will a dark and foreboding town hall send?"

"Look, I'm sorry, but we don't have the budget to replace the decorations that were ruined in the flood. I didn't ruin them," Derek said in exasperation. "And I have no choice but to work within the budget. Only a fiscally irresponsible person would do otherwise."

"What if I paid for them?" Cole asked.

Derek ran his hand through his hair, then shook his head. "Fine, whatever. As long as they look classy and not like something a kindergartner hot-glued together during craft hour." He leaned back in his chair and muttered, "I swear, this whole town's lost its mind over fairy lights and fake snow."

Grace exhaled a shaky breath and looked up at Cole with gratitude. "Thank you," she whispered.

He kissed her forehead. "Anything for you. And don't worry—we'll give your guests the winter wonderland you promised."

"Just make sure no glitter ends up in my office, or I'm filing a grievance," Derek snarked. "Now, are we finally done here?"

Grace grinned. "No promises," she snarked back. "And no, we're not done. Not until you explain why you closed the ice-skating rink."

Derek covered his face with his hands and groaned. "Not everything is about you, you know. Simply put, it's not cold enough."

"Unfortunately, he's right, darlin'," Cole informed Grace. "This time last year we were well below freezing for most of winter, not to mention all the snow. While it's been cold this year, not a single one of my ponds has come close to icing over and I doubt the one in the park has either."

"Finally, someone with some sense around here," Derek exclaimed. "And no, there is nothing we can do to fix it," he said before Grace could ask. "You're just going to have to come up with an alternate plan. One that doesn't risk the town getting sued because little Timmy fell through the ice or broke a leg or something."

Even when Derek was right, he still sounded like a jerk. "Fine," Grace replied, her voice tinged with defiance. "I just want you to know that I'm going to sign you up for every list of Christmas caroling I can find. Instead of Twelve Days of Christmas, it's going to be Twelve Days of Christmas Caroling for you."

Derek narrowed his eyes. "You wouldn't dare." He checked his calendar. "Besides that, there are only eleven days till Christmas, so you've already lost."

"I can work with that," Grace shrugged.

"You're a braver man than I am," Derek said to Cole. "Now are we finished?"

Cole looked to Grace, and when she nodded, he turned his attention back to Derek. "We'll handle the decorations from here," he informed him. "Moving forward, I assume it's not too much to ask that you inform Grace if you're going to cancel any more events that affect her?"

That wasn't a question, and by the look on Derek's face, he knew it. "Fine. I didn't realize the mayor ruled by committee in this town, but if that will keep you guys off my back and out of my office, so be it."

Grace made a 'hmmph' sound, then marched out of the office, Cole and Lyda hot on her heels. "That man," she said once they were out of earshot. "Of all the times for Mayor Allen to have an emergency, this was the worst." She grimaced as soon as the words were out of her mouth. "That sounded awful, I'm so sorry."

"It's okay," Lyda assured her. "We know what you meant." She turned toward Cole and gave him an appraising look. "So you're the infamous fiancé everyone keeps mentioning?"

A pang of jealousy washed over Grace as she watched the exchange between Cole and Lyda. Had everyone been talking about Cole, or was Lyda using that as an excuse? She wouldn't have to come up with excuses if you'd stop being insecure and remember your manners, Grace chastised herself.

Cole took Grace's hand as he tipped his hat toward Lyda. "Nice to meet you," he drawled. "Grace tells me you're opening a hat shop downtown."

"I appreciate the fact you managed to say that with a straight face," she teased. "Everyone else I've talked to has either laughed, told me I'm crazy, or both!"

"It is a bit unusual," Cole admitted. "But I'm not exactly a connoisseur of women's fashion, so what do I know?"

Lyda nodded. "I'll make sure to carry a line of cowboy hats, you know, for all the cowboys around here."

"That would be smart," Grace interjected. She cleared her throat. "I guess I better get up to the city and get those decorations before Derek changes his mind."

"If you want, I can go with you," Lyda offered.

Grace nodded. It would be incredibly rude to turn her down, and Grace had no desire to be rude to her new friend. It wasn't Lyda's fault Grace was a bit on the jealous side. "That would be great! Just give me a minute to say goodbye to Cole and I'll be ready to go."

They walked hand in hand over to his truck. "Why does it always feel like I haven't seen you in days?"

Cole leaned down and kissed her gently on the lips. "Maybe because every second apart feels like an eternity."

She smiled up at him, relieved to hear he felt the same way she did. "What are you doing in town?" Grace asked, her curiosity getting the better of her. She was definitely happy to see him but surprised at the same time. He was usually hard at work on the farm this time of day.

When they reached the truck, he turned toward her and leaned a hip up against the door. "I ran over to the hardware store for some feed," he replied. "I was planning to stop by the house to say hi when I saw your car was parked down here." He reached out and placed a hand on her hip. "I didn't mean to interrupt, but I heard y'all arguing through the window, so I thought I'd see what all the fuss was about."

"I'm glad you did," Grace replied. "Derek and I can't seem to have a conversation that doesn't devolve into a fight."

"Should I be worried about that?"

"Oh?" Grace asked, her brow raised.

Cole chuckled. "Isn't that how all those meet-cute romances start out?" he teased. "Enemies-to-lovers and all that."

In response, Grace wrapped her arms around Cole's neck and pulled his face down to hers. Then she kissed him with as much passion as she dared given they were standing on the street in front of town hall. "Does that answer your question?" she asked him when they pulled apart.

"I suppose," he drawled. "But I may need another reminder later."

Grace laughed and playfully smacked his arm. "I'll remind you as many times as you need," she teased. "Anyway, thank you for supporting me."

"Anytime, baby girl." He pulled a credit card out of his wallet and handed it to her. "Try not to go too crazy," he said, his tone changing from lighthearted to serious. "We don't want to go all *National Lampoon's Christmas Vacation* here. Even though I know that would really chap Derek's hide."

"It will be hard, but I'm sure Lyda will keep me in line," Grace replied. She looked over toward her car and saw that Lyda was waiting, her foot tapping impatiently. "I better go before she uses the 'mom voice' on me," Grace joked.

Cole gave her one last hug, then opened the door to the truck and got in. "Come by later when you're finished. The animals miss you."

"I will," she promised. She was pretty sure that was code for come snuggle in front of the fireplace while they admired the Christmas tree, and she was more than happy to comply.

Grace waved goodbye, then walked to her car. "Sorry about that," she said to Lyda. She unlocked the doors, then slid into the driver's seat. "Are you ready to shop till we drop?"

"Yes, this should be fun!" She gave Grace a sideways glance. "Any chance that man of yours has a brother?" she asked hopefully.

"Sadly, no, he's an only child," Grace said as she shook her head.

Lyda nodded. "That figures," she said with a laugh. "All the good ones are usually taken."

"Derek's still single..." Grace replied slyly. "He could use a woman like you to help him get in line."

"I always did like a challenge," Lyda joked. "I'm still not sure he'd accept a couple of rowdy boys, though."

"You never know," Grace replied. She started the car and put it in drive, then carefully pulled out onto the road. With less than three days until her guests arrived, she had a lot of work to do and little time to do it in. Her desire to play matchmaker may have to go on hold, but only temporarily. Somewhere in this town was a man for Lyda; all she had to do was find him.

-Nine-

With only two days to go until the latest batch of guests arrived, Grace was feeling her usual mix of anxiety and anticipation. There was always that tiny amount of fear present: that her guests would hate the house, hate the town, hate their room, the food, the events she planned... Thankfully, those fears were typically followed by the excitement of getting to share all the things she loves with new people. This time she was especially excited since Carl and his sister Katherine were among the guests set to arrive. She knew she could at least count on them to approve of all the hard work they'd put into this newest Experience.

"Guess what?" Rebekah called out as she entered the dining room.

"What?" Grace replied as she looked up from the ever-growing to-do list on her laptop. She'd spent the last hour breaking her list down into items grouped by order of importance, only to discover that most of them were equally important. Good thing she had help from Jilly or she'd have pulled her hair out by now.

Rebekah tossed her purse on the table and sat down. "You were supposed to guess," she teased. "But since you ruined my fun, I'll just have to tell you. I discovered there's a ski resort in a town just outside Kansas City. Since you can't do ice skating this year, you could take everyone skiing!"

Grace had lived her entire life in the Kansas City area and had never heard of a ski resort. "How is this possible? While it's true we usually get snow at least a couple of times in the winter, it usually only lasts a couple of days."

"I wondered that too, but it turns out they make their own snow using snow machines," she explained. "They offer skiing, snowboarding, and I think tubing." Rebekah shrugged. "You'd have to rent a bus to transport everyone, but I think it would be a fun way to spend a day."

"I wish I'd known about this sooner. I could have included the cost of tickets in the price of the Traditional Christmas Experience packages. I guess I'll have to eat the cost on this one."

Rebekah slid Grace's laptop across the table and, after a few moments of typing, slid it back toward Grace. "That's it," she said, pointing to the screen. "I bet they'll give you a group deal if you book in advance."

The pictures were pretty convincing that it was, in fact, a ski resort—which boggled Grace's mind. How had she never heard of this place? "Thanks, Rebekah, I'll give them a call." She picked up her phone, then put it back down at the sound of the doorbell ringing. "I wonder who that could be?" An image of Derek storming into her kitchen a couple of days before crossed her mind, and she groaned at the thought of another confrontation.

"Want me to get it?" Rebekah asked.

Grace shook her head. "I'll take care of it." If it was Derek, better to get it over with.

"By the way," Rebekah called out as Grace headed toward the door, "Town Hall looks gorgeous! You did a great job with the new decorations!"

A smile involuntarily appeared on Grace's lips. That had been mostly Lyda's doing; she had a real knack for taking things from plain to picture-perfect with just a few sprigs of pine and a string of lights. Grace had simply followed behind her, handing over bulbs and tinsel while trying not to get in the way.

Still, hearing the compliment warmed her. "Thanks," she called back over her shoulder. "I'll let Lyda know—I bet you just made her day, too!" Grace dared Derek to complain about these new decorations. Even he would be forced to admit they were the epitome of class, even if the man currently occupying the mayor's office was not.

The doorbell sounded a second time, then a third, and finally, a fourth as Grace hurried to open it. If she found Derek waiting impatiently on the other side, she was really going to give that guy a piece of her mind. "I'm coming!" she yelled as she flung open the door. "Oh," she uttered in surprise. Not only was it not Derek, it was a woman Grace had never seen before—one who was dressed like she'd taken a wrong turn in Beverly Hills only to end up in Nowhereville, Missouri. "Can I help you?"

The woman, who could easily pass for a blonde Jackie Kennedy, gave Grace a once-over, and if the look on her face was any indication, Grace did not measure up to her standards.

"Is this the," she held her phone out in front of her and stared at the screen for a moment, "Enchanted Holiday Hideaway Bed and Breakfast?"

"Yes, it is," Grace said hesitantly. Was this woman one of her guests? It wasn't exactly uncommon for at least one of them to arrive early. "Are you here for the Traditional Christmas Experience?"

She wrinkled her nose in distaste. "No," she said as she handed Grace a set of car keys. "The luggage is in the trunk. Please see that it makes it to my room." She then sauntered past Grace into the foyer, shaking her head as she took in the details.

Grace followed her back inside. "Ma'am, I think there's been some sort of mistake, I—"

"Grace, who's at the door?" Rebekah called out. "I swear I heard my—" She paused in the doorway as soon as she saw the woman. "Oh my gosh, Mom!"

That stopped Grace in her tracks. This woman was Rebekah's mom? Now that she saw them side by side, she supposed she could see the resemblance. "You never told me your mom was coming," Grace accused.

"That's because I had no idea," Rebekah replied, a bewildered look on her face. She turned to her mom. "What are you doing here?"

"I've come to put an end to this nonsense and take you back home," she sniffed. She gave Rebekah an appraising glance and then gave her the same look she'd given Grace. "What happened to you? You look like, well, you look like her," she said, pointing to Grace.

Rebekah and Grace both looked down at their jeans and sweaters and then back up at each other. "What's wrong with how we're dressed?" Rebekah asked.

"If I have to explain that to you, things are clearly much worse than even I imagined." She pulled a credit card out of her purse and handed it to Grace. "I'll take your best room, and don't forget about my luggage; I would like to freshen up and expect to find it in my room as soon as I get there."

Grace's eyes widened as she looked to Rebekah for help. "Ma'am, we're completely booked up for the holidays."

"Then bump someone," she said dismissively.

"I can't," Grace tried to explain. "They've already paid and—"

The woman waved her hand as if to shoo Grace away. "If the Waldorf can make space, surely someone of your... stature can, too."

"Mom, this is a waste of time," Rebekah hurried to say. "I'm not going back to New York with you, now or ever. So why don't you save yourself the trouble and go back home."

"I promised your father I would not return without you," she said stubbornly. "So, if you want me to leave, I suggest you get packing. Otherwise, I'll take that room."

Rebekah sighed, then turned to Grace. "She can have my room," she said begrudgingly. "But you should definitely charge her for it. And make sure to add on a nuisance tax," she gave her mother one of her own withering looks, "because I can guarantee she is going to be a nuisance."

"Even worse than you were last Valentine's Day?" Grace teased. She immediately regretted those words. This was clearly not the time for jokes.

"You've spent way too much time with these country bumpkins," the woman chided. "There was a time when you would have never dared to speak of your mother like that. I'm disappointed in you," she shook her head in dismay.

Grace had never been called a country bumpkin before. Should she be insulted? It sounded like an insult. "Um, I'll go get your luggage," Grace said, excusing herself from the awkward mother-daughter conversation.

When she stepped out onto the porch, she half expected to find a limousine and driver waiting and was a little disappointed to find a classy Cadillac instead. Not that she should have been surprised, though she did wonder where it had come from. Did rental cars come in luxury editions? She honestly didn't know; she'd never rented a car before.

With a sigh, she wandered over to the trunk and used the key fob to pop it open, sighing even harder once she saw the contents. "How long did this woman plan to stay?" Grace muttered. This was going to require at least two trips—she tugged on the first suitcase—and maybe the assistance of a couple of linebackers. How had Rebekah's mom gotten these in the trunk? *She probably ordered some poor guy to do it for her,* Grace thought, somewhat uncharitably.

Since there was no way she'd be lifting the suitcase by herself, she focused on the smaller carry-on bags and then made her way up to Rebekah's room. Now that Rebekah had been displaced, they would have to figure out new sleeping arrangements. Especially if Grace still planned to give up her room to some of the other guests.

As soon as she reached the door, she paused when she heard voices. It was rude to eavesdrop, but Grace couldn't seem to help herself.

"I still don't understand why you're here," Rebekah said, her voice laced with exasperation. "You made it very clear last May that I was out of the family."

Grace peeked through the door and saw Rebekah flinging clothes haphazardly into a duffel bag.

"Neither your father nor I expected you to disobey us," her mom replied nonchalantly. "But since you were clearly in your 'rebellious' phase, we decided to give you some time to experience the reality of life on your own. I must say, I expected you to cave within the first week. You must get that stubborn streak from your father."

Rebekah stopped packing and faced her mother. "You know, I was surprised at how well I was able to adapt, too. But once I realized what I was really capable of, I discovered I didn't need your money to be happy. In fact, I don't think I've ever been happier in my entire life."

Her mother scoffed. "You can't be serious." She waved her hand around the room. "Your closet back home is bigger than this entire room, for crying out loud. And look at you, dressed like a street urchin," she shuddered. "My daughter would never be caught dead wearing anything less than the newest fashions."

"Maybe that was true of the 'old' Rebekah, but the new one realized months ago she didn't need designer clothes, or the newest phone, or to frequent the trendiest restaurants. I have a life now, Mom. A real life. That doesn't revolve around money or social status."

"This is my fault," she replied. "I told your father we were being too harsh, but you know how he is. Now look at you, you've spent so much time with these 'creatures' you've come to believe you're one of them." She shook her head and sighed dramatically as she flopped back against the pillows. Moments later, she snapped her fingers and sat up. "I know what you need. You need to be reminded of what you've lost. I'll book us a spa day for tomorrow. We'll get your hair and nails done, shop for a proper wardrobe, and have lunch at the finest restaurant Kansas City has to offer." She paused briefly. "Surely there are places around here that can accommodate us. I'll ask the maid, though I doubt she knows. She looks like she's never seen the inside of a hair salon. Seriously, does she cut her hair with a weed whacker?"

Grace's hand subconsciously reached up to touch her hair. Did it really look that bad? And if it did, why didn't anyone ever tell her? Surely, at least one of her so-called friends was bold enough to tell her the truth. One of them was a hairstylist, for Pete's sake.

"Mom!" Rebekah admonished. "Don't talk about Grace like that. She was the only one who stood by me when my entire family disowned me, and she does not deserve to be treated with anything less than the utmost respect and kindness."

While Grace appreciated Rebekah defending her, she couldn't help but notice she hadn't denied her mother's claims. She would need to book an appointment with Evie ASAP. And maybe have a word with those who had spent the last year letting her run around looking like Bozo the Clown.

Before things could get any worse, she knocked on the door and then entered the room without waiting for an invitation. "Here are your bags," she said as she set them down in the corner. "I still need to get your suitcase, but since it's a little on the heavy side, I'll have to wait for some help to get it up the stairs."

"I'll help you," Rebekah volunteered. "By the way, this is Jacqueline Rutherford," Rebekah said by way of introductions. "Feel free to call her Jackie."

Interesting. Hadn't Grace just compared her to Jackie Kennedy? What a coincidence they shared the same name.

"Don't you dare," Jackie spat. She narrowed her eyes at Rebekah. "You know darn well I hate that name."

"Yes, I do," Rebekah said cheerfully. "Which is why I'll be telling everyone I see to call you that."

"What did I do to deserve such disrespect?" Jackie muttered. "For nine months I carried you, and this is the thanks I get," she clucked her tongue, then turned her ire toward Grace. "And you, I thought I told you I wanted your best room. Surely this," she swept her arm to encompass the room, "is not the best you have to offer."

Grace couldn't help but note that Valerie and her mother hadn't been this demanding, although Rebekah had just warned her. "I'm sorry, but this is the best I can do on such short notice. Dinner will be at six, the bathroom is right across the hall, and we have an assortment of drinks and snacks on hand at all times." She turned to Rebekah with a pleading look. "We should go get your mom's suitcase."

Rebekah nodded. "We'll be right back. Please try not to cause any drama in the meantime."

"Yeah right, and how would I do that? There's no one here but me and the dust bunnies."

Grace opened her mouth to protest. They worked really hard to keep the house a dust bunny-free zone, and frankly, that comment was more offensive than the weed whacker one. But before she could say something to defend herself, Rebekah shoved her out the door.

"It's not worth it," she whispered. She grabbed Grace's hand and dragged her down the stairs and out to her mom's car. "I'm really sorry about this," she said as she assessed the luggage still in the trunk. "Never in my wildest dreams, or nightmares, could I have ever expected my mother to step foot in this town."

"It doesn't seem likely Winterwood would make the list of possible vacation destinations," Grace agreed.

Rebekah gave her a sideways glance and laughed. "I appreciate your ability to keep your sense of humor in these trying times. I promise I will do everything I can to get rid of her as quickly as possible."

"Are you sure you want to do that?" Grace hesitated to ask. "It wasn't that long ago you wished for an opportunity to reconnect with your mom."

"If you're referring to the comment I made after Amelia Parrish left at Thanksgiving, you forgot the part where I wished my mom would have a change of heart like Amelia had. I think it's pretty clear that hasn't happened."

"Maybe she just needs a chance to realize the error of her ways?" Grace asked hopefully.

Rebekah snorted. "It would take a miracle."

"Good thing 'tis the season of miracles, then," Grace replied.

After a ton of grunting, groaning, and straining, they managed to lift the suitcase out of the trunk. "What's in here, cement?" Grace asked as she wiped the sweat from her brow.

"You never know," Rebekah joked. "But I wouldn't be surprised if she brought half her shoe collection."

Grace's eyes went wide. "Are her shoes made of cement?"

Rebekah laughed as she shook her head. "Let's get this upstairs before we pass out from exhaustion."

It took them a good ten minutes, but they managed to get the suitcase to Rebekah's room. When they finally deposited it in the corner with the rest of the bags, Jackie handed Grace a couple of dollars for her effort. It felt like more of an insult than a tip, but Grace decided to go the 'kill-them-with-kindness' route and simply smiled wide and mumbled a polite 'thank you' before leaving them alone once more. It was going to be a long couple of days; she could feel it in her bones.

-Eight-

Less than twenty-four hours had passed since Rebekah's mother had first appeared, and Grace was already ready to send her back to New York. She had complained non-stop the entire time she'd been there. The towels weren't soft enough, the thread count on the sheets wasn't high enough, the comforter wasn't plush enough, there weren't enough pillows, the pillows weren't fluffy enough, the mattress wasn't firm enough—and on and on and on she went. Did the Waldorf put up with this? Or were they perfect? Grace honestly wasn't sure a level of perfection existed for Jacqueline Rutherford.

Then there was the food. The look on Jackie's face when Grace had informed her they did not, in fact, have prime rib would have been comical if it hadn't been followed by a tantrum the likes of which Grace had never seen before. She had been on the verge of joining Jackie in said tantrum when Rebekah had arrived and offered to take her mother to a restaurant in the city. At this point, Grace had no idea how the rest of the night had gone since she'd gone the way of the coward and hightailed it to Cole's the second she'd gotten Granny settled for the night.

Which brought her to now, where she found herself in her kitchen, at six-thirty in the morning, scrolling through fine dining breakfast ideas. Grace knew her efforts were likely in vain, but she was determined to wipe the haughty look off her guest's face—or she'd die trying. Unfortunately, too many of these recipes required ingredients she'd not only never heard of but had no idea how to acquire. So much for operation 'haughty look'; it was time for Plan B.

"What are you doing?" Rebekah asked quietly from her position just outside the door.

Grace looked up at the sound of Rebekah's voice but had to crane her neck to spot her. "A better question is, what are you doing?" Grace asked in confusion. "Is there a reason you're hiding behind that door?"

Rebekah slowly walked into the room, then over to the breakfast bar, where she hesitated for just a moment before taking a seat. "On a scale of one to ten, how mad at me are you?" she asked with a sigh.

"Why would I be mad at you?" Grace put down her tablet and gave Rebekah her full attention.

"Seriously?" she replied, her tone full of sarcasm. "Do I really need to list all the mom-sized reasons you likely hate my guts right now?"

"That's a tad...extreme," Grace drawled. "It's not your fault your mom showed up unexpectedly, nor is it your fault she's a bit on the demanding side."

"A bit?" Rebekah raised a brow.

"Okay, fine, a ton, but again, that's not your fault." Grace leaned on the counter and sighed. "Look, I'm not even the slightest bit mad at you, but I am concerned. Our guests are set to arrive tomorrow, and I can't have your mother pitching a fit every time I fail to live up to her impossibly high standards—which I'm likely to do at every turn. Is there any way we can convince her to go home? Or at least to a hotel?"

Rebekah shook her head. "I've already tried, but she's refusing to leave without me." She closed her eyes and shook her head. "I can't do it," she whispered.

Grace reached across the counter and clasped Rebekah's hands. "It's okay, we'll figure something out. In the meantime," Grace said in a cheerful voice, "I'm trying to come up with a breakfast plan that will impress the unimpressible. Do you have any ideas?"

She shook her head and gave Grace a pained look. "I'm sorry, I should have talked to you about that last night. My mom won't be down until at least ten, and then she only takes a cup of tea and one piece of toast with jam. There's a bag in the pantry with the supplies I bought last night."

Grace walked over to the pantry to look for the items, and sure enough, a bag was sitting on one of the shelves. How she'd managed to miss it the ten or so times she'd rummaged through there this morning was beyond her. Out of curiosity, she looked in the bag and found a fancy container full of expensive-sounding tea and a jar of peach marmalade. She then held up the jar for Rebekah to see. "This doesn't look high-end enough," she teased.

Rebekah rolled her eyes. "Don't get me started, okay? We must have stopped at every grocery store between here and Kansas City before Mom finally agreed—begrudgingly, I might add—on that one. And I'm lucky she agreed to that." She gave Grace a sheepish look. "We never got a chance to talk about sleeping arrangements."

"I don't like the way you're looking at me," Grace said nervously.

"Wellll," Rebekah drawled out, "it's just that, since Mom took over my room, I figured I'd crash with Thorne. To make it easier," she hurried to add.

"So you want to leave me here alone with your mother?"

Rebekah couldn't meet Grace's eyes. "I'm hoping this might make her give up quicker."

"That's your excuse?" Grace asked, barely able to contain her laughter. "Surely you can come up with a better reason than that for wanting to move in with your boyfriend!"

"I'm not moving in with him," Rebekah protested. "I just thought it would make things easier. I'm assuming you plan to move to Cole's while the guests are here, and I really don't want to crowd you again like I did at Thanksgiving."

"I appreciate that, but I never felt crowded. Not only that, someone has to be here in case the guests need something during the night, so I might end up crashing on the couch in the living room, or maybe even on an air mattress in Granny's room. Regardless, you have my blessing to move to Thorne's. I suppose I'll survive."

"Thanks," Rebekah said, her voice full of gratitude. "If you change your mind, let me know, and we can make a pillow fort or something!"

Grace smiled and rolled her eyes. "I might just do that," she teased. "Anyway, I better get to work on the usual slop I normally make for breakfast. Seeing as I no longer need to impress your mom, it's back to eggs and bacon!"

"You'll get no complaints from me!"

***

Grace had just finished cleaning the kitchen when Jackie appeared for her tea and toast. She was dressed in a black pantsuit with a cashmere sweater, silk scarf, and ankle boots, and Grace couldn't help but wonder if Jackie always dressed like that, or if she planned to visit the local country club. Because if not, she was way overdressed for hanging out at a small-town B&B for the day.

"I'll have your tea and toast ready in a jiffy!" Grace called out with an enthusiasm she did not feel. "Please feel free to have a seat wherever you're most comfortable."

Jackie raised a perfectly manicured brow. "I would be most comfortable at home," she replied in an accusing tone.

"I would be happy to help you arrange that," Grace said brightly.

"Good. All you need to do is kick Rebekah out, and we will both be on our way."

Grace jerked to a stop and almost dropped the jar of marmalade she was carrying. "I'm sorry, I don't think I heard you correctly. Can you repeat that?"

"You heard me," Jackie stated in a tone that brokered no argument. "Rebekah does not belong here, but as long as you're willing to play the part of her caretaker, she will refuse to see reason."

This woman had a lot of nerve, and Grace seriously wondered how Rebekah had managed to avoid turning out like her mother. In this case, the apple DID fall far from the tree.

"First of all, I am not Rebekah's caretaker, and it is a huge insult to your daughter to imply she is incapable of taking care of herself—which she most definitely can and is. Second, I am not going to kick out my best friend just so you can try to force her back into a life she doesn't want. And third, even if I did kick her out, she still has options other than returning to New York." Grace paused to take a breath, but judging by the look on Jackie's face, her words were not hitting home like she hoped. "What happened to a parent wanting their kid to be happy? Isn't that important to you?"

Jackie raised her chin and sniffed. "Of course I want my daughter to be happy. That's the very reason I'm here—to take her home, where she belongs, so she can be happy."

"You mean, so you can be happy," Grace corrected.

"A mother knows what's best for her kids. When you have kids of your own, you'll understand."

Out of curiosity, Grace decided to explore that line of thought. "Okay, I'll bite. Why do you think Rebekah would be happier in New York than she is here?"

"Are you serious? How could she possibly be happy wilting away in a town like this? Rebekah is a woman of the world—a socialite born and bred to be social. What she is not is some backwoods, overalls-wearing, shoeless hillbilly." She looked down her nose at Grace. "No offense."

Grace looked down at her socks and then up at Jackie. It was clear Jackie was talking about her, and that she did mean offense. "Rebekah has her own wedding and event planning business," Grace informed her. "So, she's not exactly spending her time milking cows and mucking out stalls." Grace managed to refrain from tacking on "like me" at the end. Jackie already thought so little of her—no need to give her more ammo or stereotypes to use against her.

Jackie paused briefly to consider the new piece of information. "I suppose that's not entirely awful," she ground out. "But still nothing compared to the life she could and should have back home."

"Why now?" Grace blurted out. Seven months had passed since Rebekah's parents had pretty much disowned her, and to Grace's knowledge, they hadn't checked in with her once in all that time. Something had changed—Grace just needed time to figure out what.

"I'll take my tea in my room." With that, Jackie turned on her heel and stomped out of the room.

Grace watched Jackie go, the feeling that something more was going on getting stronger with each second. She did not have time for a mystery, but it looked like she would have to make time. Rebekah's happiness may just depend on it.

***

After a very trying day, Grace found herself wandering around town looking at all the Christmas lights. The townsfolk had really outdone themselves this year, every building, every home, every lamppost in the downtown area was covered in lights. It was beautiful, and she couldn't wait to see the expression on her guests' faces when she brought them here to see it.

When she reached the town hall, despite the cold, she sat down on the bench and stared off into space as she tried to figure out what her next steps should be in the ongoing Jackie and Rebekah saga.

"Is this a new way of haunting me?" a voice called out.

Grace jumped and turned to see Derek standing behind her. "You're the one who just scared me," she admonished. She checked her watch and saw that it was after seven. "Shouldn't you be home by now? I can't imagine a town this size requiring the mayor to work overtime."

"You seem to forget that I neither live nor work here," he reminded her. "So, I'm forced to work around my busy schedule, which sometimes requires late nights."

It was true that she had forgotten that, and for a moment, she felt sorry for him. He had been asked to completely upend his life for a town—and its people—he no longer had a connection to. And here he was, dutifully working late on top of it all.

"Why are you here?" he asked.

"Can't a girl admire some Christmas lights?" she replied, a tad defensively.

Derek raised a brow. "Don't you have your own lights to admire?"

"Technically, these are my lights since my husband is the one who paid for them," she snapped.

"Don't you mean fiancé?" he said sarcastically. "Or did I manage to miss the big wedding?"

Grace rolled her eyes. "Fine, fiancé, whatever," she snarked. "Anyway, since it's apparently now a crime to sit on a bench and look at lights, I will leave you to your work." She stood and prepared to stomp off, briefly wishing she had a door to slam, but before she could make her dramatic exit, he grabbed her arm and stopped her.

"Look, I'm sorry," he said with a sigh. "Today was stressful, and I'm taking it out on you—mostly because you're here. Feel free to stay as long as you want, although I don't buy your excuse that you're just 'admiring the lights'."

"I accept your apology," Grace replied, somewhat pacified. "And you're right, I'm down here because I'm hiding from my guest. Some hostess I am," she said dryly.

Derek took a seat on the bench and motioned for her to join him. "Want to talk about it? I could use the distraction."

Did she want to talk about it? To him of all people? She decided she might as well, after all, maybe it would help to get an outside opinion. Even if that opinion came from someone who actively disliked her.

"If there's a female version of Scrooge, she's currently staying at my house," Grace began, some of the tension loosening from her shoulders as she voiced the thoughts she'd been holding back for the last two days. "My actual guests arrive tomorrow, and I'm terrified she's going to ruin Christmas for them."

"So why not ask her to leave?" he replied. "You're running a business, and as a business owner, you have the right to refuse service."

"Because she's Rebekah's mom," Grace explained. "And there's a part of me that's hoping if I let her stay, a miracle will happen and she'll make amends with her daughter."

Derek nodded slowly as he listened. "I can see that, but you can't let a dream ruin your reality."

"That sounded very wise and yet cryptic," Grace teased.

"I guess it did," he said with a laugh. "I just meant the dream is nice, but it might not come true."

"So don't let the possibility of something that might not happen ruin actual plans?"

"Exactly!"

He was right, but that didn't make things any easier.

"We all want to be liked, Grace," Derek said gently, "but when you're a business owner, or an acting mayor, sometimes you have to do the hard job of saying no and setting boundaries. It doesn't make you a bad guy, it's just part of the job."

Once again, he was right, and she wasn't sure how to feel about it. She'd become so used to everyone loving her ideas, she'd never learned how to graciously accept that some people may not like them. "You're right," she admitted. "I know that was partly directed toward me, and I'm sorry."

Derek stood up and stretched. "It's okay. It's been a difficult time for both of us." He looked around at the lights. "I must admit, you did do a good job."

"You have Lyda to thank for this," Grace said, waving her hand to encompass the decorations. "She's single, by the way."

He raised both brows in surprise. "You must not like her very much if you're trying to play matchmaker with me."

Grace shrugged. "Just because we don't get along doesn't mean you and Lyda wouldn't."

"Well, I will keep that in mind. But once again, I don't live here, so..."

"The city isn't that far," Grace laughed. "It's only forty-five minutes away, not forty-five hours."

Derek snorted. "You try making the trip multiple times a day and then come talk to me."

"Fine," Grace said as she rolled her eyes. "Who knows, maybe you'll end up moving back here. You wouldn't be the first."

"Never going to happen," Derek said sternly.

Grace stood and smiled sweetly at him. "Famous last words!" She took off before he could reply, leaving him with a disgruntled look on his face. Oh well, she'd planted a seed in regards to Lyda, what happened next was out of her hands.

-Seven-

"The big day is finally here!" Grace announced excitedly at breakfast. She looked around at Molly, Grant, Emilio, Granny, and Gladys, and then made a show of checking her watch. "Any minute now our first guest will arrive and our Traditional Christmas Experience will officially begin!"

Molly looked up from her pancakes, a tired expression on her normally cheerful face. "Do you have a plan for how to deal with Grumpy Claus and keep her from ruining Christmas?" Molly asked, her head nodding toward the stairs and indicating Jackie.

Grace shook her head, her excitement dimming at the mention of her unexpected house guest. "My hope is she will choose to avoid the festivities, and the problem will solve itself. If that doesn't happen, I guess I'll have to ask her to leave."

Granny reached across the table and patted Grace's hand. "Grace dear, you know we can't kick out Rebekah's mother. Not when there's still a chance—"

"—A chance for what?" Rebekah asked from the doorway.

All eyes turned toward Rebekah, as none of them had noticed her come in.

"A chance for reconciliation," Granny said firmly.

"I see," Rebekah said slowly. "Well, that is certainly news to me. From what I've heard, my mom has been campaigning to get me kicked out of here. I could be wrong, but those don't appear to be the actions of someone looking to reconcile."

Granny and Gladys exchanged a look. "I didn't realize..." Granny trailed off.

"It's okay," Rebekah assured her. "I appreciate you looking out for me, but when it comes to my mom, I think it's best we treat her exactly like we would any guest who causes trouble. Please don't give her special treatment because of me."

Emilio cleared his throat. "As someone with experience in the 'difficult mother' camp, let me give you some advice: set boundaries and enforce them swiftly. It's hard, but it's the only way to save your sanity."

Rebekah gave Emilio a compassionate look. "You're right. I will have a conversation with my mom as soon as she gets up. If we're lucky, she'll be on her way to the airport before the first guest arrives."

The doorbell rang, causing everyone to jump at the unexpected noise. "I'll get that," Grace called out with a laugh. "There's plenty of pancakes, help yourself," she said to Rebekah as she passed her on the way to the door.

Once she was alone in the foyer, Grace paused to take a breath as a mixture of excitement and anxiety bubbled to the surface. She loved meeting her guests but wished she could skip the awkward introductions where she never quite knew what to say. As soon as she felt composed, she pasted a smile on her face and threw open the door, only to find one very handsome cowboy instead of her guests.

"Cole!" she exclaimed as she launched herself into his waiting arms. "What are you doing ringing the doorbell, silly? You should know by now you can just walk in."

"I know," he said with a chuckle. "But I was hoping to get you alone, and this seemed like a good way to do it." He leaned down to kiss her, his arms tightening around her waist. Moments later, he pulled back and smiled down at her. "I don't have a lot of time; I just wanted to wish you luck with your guests."

He really was the best, wasn't he? "You're so sweet," she said as she kissed him again. "And thoughtful," she kissed him a second time. "And I love you!"

"I love you, too!" he replied. "Any chance I'll see you later tonight?"

Grace nodded enthusiastically. "Wild horses couldn't keep me away!"

Cole laughed. "I'm glad to hear it. I could use some help wrangling the furball."

"Oh?" Grace raised her brow, certain she knew which furball he was referring to. "I'm assuming Piper is still giving you trouble with the Christmas tree?"

"I spent thirty minutes searching for her this morning, only to discover her hidden in the branches at the top of the tree." He shook his head in bewilderment. "I have no idea how that tiny kitten managed to get all the way up there but keeping her out of the tree has become an exercise in futility."

Grace smiled at the image. "Next time, I guess you'll have to check the tree first!"

"I guess I should have done that this morning. I just thought she'd be a lot easier to spot." His expression changed from amused to serious. "I had started to fear she'd escaped the house..." he trailed off and sighed. "Anyway, all that's to say that we miss you and are looking forward to seeing you later tonight."

"I promise to give her a stern talking-to when I get there," Grace teased. When he smiled, she breathed an inward sigh of relief. She knew it had really bothered him to think he might have to tell her Piper was missing—or worse—and she felt terrible for putting him in that position, even though they'd both agreed it was best to leave the animals with him. This whole back-and-forth living situation was getting to everyone, and they really needed to come to a decision once and for all. But that was a problem for another day. How many times had she thought that recently? When that day finally arrived, she was going to be in big trouble.

The sound of a car horn caught their attention, and they turned to see Carl and his sister Katherine waving from the side of the road.

"Looks like I got here just in time," Cole whispered as they waved back.

"And now you have to leave," Grace stated as a wave of disappointment washed over her.

Cole leaned down to kiss her one last time. "Yes, but don't forget we'll be together again later tonight." Before she could reply, he sauntered off down the steps, walked over to Carl, and shook his hand. He then waved goodbye to Grace and continued over to his truck, waving one last time before driving off.

As soon as Cole was out of sight, Grace snapped out of her daze and hurried over to greet Carl and Katherine. "I'm so excited to see you both again," she said, giving each of them a hug. "How have you been? How was your trip? Here, let me help with those," she said as she grabbed a couple of their bags.

Carl laughed as he picked up the remaining bags. "It's good to see you, too, Grace," he replied. He nudged Katherine with his elbow. "How have we been?"

Katherine rolled her eyes and playfully nudged him back. "I'd say we're doing as well as a couple of old codgers possibly could!"

Grace smiled as she led them into the house. "I'm pretty sure everyone is still in the dining room if you want to say hi before I take you to your room," she informed them. "Or, you can go to your room first and get settled before facing the rest of the gang. I just know they're going to have a thousand questions."

"Um, how about we get settled first, and then we'll join you in the dining room?" Katherine replied. "Even though we flew in last night, the hour-and-a-half drive to get here this morning has left me feeling a little less than fresh, if you know what I mean."

"That sounds good. I'll have coffee, tea, and pastries waiting for you."

Since Carl and Katherine had stayed there last Christmas, Grace felt comfortable skipping the tour she usually gave her guests and led them directly to their room. She then left them there to get situated while she returned to the dining room, only to discover that Jackie had come down early and was now engaged in a heated discussion with Rebekah while the rest of the group looked on in stunned silence.

"I am not leaving this house without you, young lady, and that is final," Jackie said vehemently. "May I remind you that you have a duty to your father and me, and we expect you to honor it."

Rebekah stepped forward until she was nose to nose with her mother. "I am a human being with my own life, NOT some object you can own and do with as you please. Not only am I not leaving here with you, you can take your duty and honor and shove it." She then turned on her heel and stomped out of the room. Seconds later, the sound of the front door slamming caused them all to jump.

"Um," Grace said nervously. Had Carl and Katherine overheard that? She hoped not, but since their room was above the dining room, it seemed impossible that they had not.

Jackie turned to Grace and glared at her. "None of this would be happening if you would just do what I asked." Without waiting for a reply, she shoved past Grace, stomped her way up the stairs, then slammed the door to her room.

Grace bowed her head and squeezed her eyes shut. This was even worse than she had imagined. "What are we going to do?" she whispered to no one in particular.

Molly stood and gave Grace a side hug. "This isn't your fault," she assured Grace. "Maybe we could convince Jackie to move to the hotel if we promise her a presidential suite."

"But we don't have a presidential suite," Grace protested. "And she just refused to leave the house without Rebekah. There's no way she'll fall for that; she'll just assume this is our way of getting her out."

"Let's just give everyone time to calm down," Granny said calmly. "Did I hear you come in with someone?" she asked Grace.

Grace nodded, her arm still tightly wrapped around Molly's waist. "Carl and Katherine just arrived. They'll be down shortly to see everyone."

Molly exchanged looks with Grant. "Think we can put off going to the office for a little while longer?" she asked her husband. "I would love to introduce Carl and Katherine to Eliza."

"Of course, dear," Grant replied.

The doorbell rang a second time, and Grace hurried to answer it. This time, she skipped the calming breath, preferring to get the newest arrivals to their room before any more drama erupted. When she opened the door, she found a young couple waiting for her on the other side.

"Hello," Grace said warmly. "You must be Ross and Megan!"

The couple smiled back, their faces practically glowing as they stood there in each other's embrace. "And you must be Grace," Megan said cheerfully. "We are so excited to be here!"

Grace briefly wondered why they were spending Christmas with her and not with their families, but quickly pushed that thought aside. It was none of her business. So, she reached down to grab a couple of their bags and motioned for them to follow her inside. She then cautiously led them upstairs and to their room, practically tiptoeing past Jackie's door so as not to alert her to their presence, lest she decide to make another scene.

"This is your room," Grace said as she opened the door with a flourish. She watched their reactions carefully, all the while hoping they would love the room as much as she did. From the inviting fire in the corner, to the canopy bed decked out with Christmas-themed bedding, to the Christmas tree just waiting for their personal touches. She believed she'd thought of everything, and if she'd forgotten something, she hoped the gift basket full of champagne, chocolate-covered strawberries, assorted teas, coffees, and hot chocolates would make up for it.

"It's perfect!" Megan exclaimed, her eyes wide with excitement. She threw her arms around Ross's neck and kissed his cheek. "Don't you just love it!"

Ross squeezed her waist and nodded his agreement. He then moved into the room and began to unpack their bags.

Grace took that as her cue to leave. "There will be drinks and appetizers available in the dining room if you want to come down and meet some of the other guests," Grace informed them. "Otherwise, lunch will be served around noon." She then shut the door and made her way back downstairs, just as the doorbell rang for a third time. She checked her watch, surprised to see that it was after eleven. Where had the time gone?

When she opened the door, she came face-to-face with a man, woman, baby, and what looked like every baby item ever made. How they had managed to fit all that in their car was beyond her. How they were going to fit it all in their room was a mystery. As far as Grace could tell, there was a highchair, a portable crib, a walker, a baby swing, a bag full of toys and stuffed animals, multiple suitcases, and a car seat.

"Babies require a lot of stuff," the woman said sheepishly.

At the sound of the woman's voice, Grace remembered her manners and smiled. "Forgive me, I was just surprised," Grace said as she awkwardly chuckled. She held out her hand. "You must be Arnie and Louisa, and this must be baby Rosalyn," Grace said, shaking the infant's hand. The little girl looked up at Grace and gurgled, completely melting Grace's heart. "Please come in." She stepped out onto the porch and began to pick up as many items as she felt she could safely carry up the stairs.

Just as she was getting ready to follow them inside, Grace noticed a minivan pulling into the driveway and groaned. Apparently, all her guests had decided to arrive at the same time. Had that ever happened before? She couldn't remember, but she was pretty sure the answer was no.

When the man she assumed was Teddy opened his door, Grace called out to him. "I'll be right with you!" She then hurried inside to show Arnie and Louisa to their room, praying all the way there was enough space to house them and all their belongings.

As soon as she opened the door, Louisa squealed in excitement, which Grace considered to be a good sign.

"This has got to be the most adorable bed and breakfast we've ever stayed at!" Louisa exclaimed. "Look," she said to Arnie as she pointed to the fireplace. "An actual working fireplace! And look at the bedding, it's so...Christmassy!"

"I am so glad you like it," Grace replied. She tried not to sound as relieved as she felt. "I need to go greet the next guests, but there are drinks and appetizers in the dining room if you want to come down and mingle with the other guests. Lunch will be at noon, and dinner will be at six. If you need anything, just let me know!" She then shut the door and took off at a jog down the stairs and back to the porch, where the last batch of guests were now waiting.

"I'm so sorry to keep you waiting," Grace replied between breaths. Man, she really needed to work out more if a couple of quick trips up and down the stairs caused her to get this winded. "You must be Teddy, Hannah, Leo, Leora, and baby Lexi," Grace said as she shook each of their hands. She couldn't help but notice that the family had a lot less luggage than Arnie and Louisa, despite also having a baby and two extra kids. Maybe things changed once you got around to baby number three. "Please follow me," Grace said as she grabbed a couple of bags.

She led them to the top of the stairs and then into the biggest bedroom on the floor. "Do you think this room will be big enough for all of you?"

Hannah looked around as she bit her bottom lip. "It's possible," she said hesitantly. She then straightened her shoulders and nodded. "We'll make it work."

"I have an idea I'd like to share with you in private," Grace informed her. "But I should let you get settled." She gave them the same spiel she'd given everyone else, then turned to leave, closing the door behind her.

Once she was safely in the hall, Grace leaned against the wall for a moment to catch her breath. The guests had arrived, and everyone seemed to be happy. Now all she had to do was keep them that way. Grace eyed Jackie's door and sighed: Easier said than done.

-Six-

For the first time in what, six months? Grace found herself awake all night. Was she exhausted? Yes, but that apparently meant nothing to her restless and overactive mind.

The day before had gone about as well as could be expected. Jackie had mercifully decided to spend the day in her room, yet every time Grace had passed her door, she had heard Jackie talking to someone. Jackie was clearly plotting something, and Grace was certain nothing good would come of it.

Then there was Hannah and Teddy. They had been thrilled with Grace's offer to give the twins, Leo and Leora, a separate room so the family had more space. But that had meant Grace was left with nowhere to sleep but the couch in the living room, hence her current situation of being awake at three in the morning.

Since no amount of sheep counting, pleas, or clock watching appeared to work, she decided to make herself a cup of hot chocolate and do a little snooping. Thankfully, she had brought her laptop down when she moved her things out of her bedroom upstairs. Once she had her beverage, she hunkered down on the couch under her blankets and set to work.

First, she did a quick social media search of Rebekah's name, but all that resulted in were posts showcasing some of the recent weddings and events she'd planned. Next, she did a search for Jackie, but all that netted was a few mentions on what looked to be her friend's accounts. Apparently Jackie didn't use social media. Since social media was a bust, Grace decided to do an internet search. She typed in Rebekah's name, as well as New York City, and then waited for the results, inhaling sharply as numerous articles flooded the page.

As she scrolled through the junk, an article from a newspaper caught her eye, and Grace quickly clicked the link.

Mr. and Mrs. Harvey Rutherford of New York City, New York are pleased to announce the engagement of Rebekah Rutherford to Thomas Haverford, a lawyer from Connecticut.

"Oh my gosh!" Grace gasped. This had to be why Jackie insisted Rebekah return to New York with her, she was planning Rebekah's wedding! This was absolutely insane. Did Rebekah even know this man? Well, now that the mystery of Jackie's sudden appearance had been solved, what were they supposed to do now? And how on earth was Grace supposed to sleep now that she'd stumbled across this particular bomb?

She took another sip of her hot chocolate and winced, the hot beverage had managed to turn ice cold in the time it had taken her to do her search. Oh well, she would just have to go back to counting sheep and barring that, hope the hours would pass quickly until she could talk to Rebekah.

***

To her surprise, Grace had managed to fall asleep quickly after the big revelation hours before. That had been the easy part; the hard part was keeping the news to herself until she could get Rebekah alone. Rebekah, who was still staying with Thorne and might not even show up that day. With that in mind, Grace sent her a text asking her to stop by at breakfast time, then promptly forgot about it as she struggled to get breakfast for twenty people on the table.

Just as Grace had set the last plate of scrambled eggs on the buffet, Jilly came rushing into the room.

"I'm so sorry I'm late," Jilly called out, her eyes wide and her expression frazzled. "My daughter got gum stuck in her hair and while I was dealing with that, my son decided that was the perfect time to feed Froot Loops to my grandparents' dog, who then promptly threw up all over the living room carpet." She paused to take a deep breath and look around. "It looks like you already made breakfast," she said, a crestfallen look washing over her face.

To be honest, Grace had forgotten Jilly was supposed to cook the meals, and more importantly, why. The lack of sleep and shocking news was obviously getting to her since Jilly had been there most of yesterday catering for her guests. In a moment of sheer panic, Grace carefully eyed the breakfast foods, and to her relief, saw that every dish was gluten-free, minus the toast, which could easily be set aside.

"It's okay," Grace assured Jilly. "I did the best I could, but it would be great if you could check everything to make sure it's safe and then fill in any of the gaps I may have created in my haste."

"Of course, I'll get right on it."

Guests slowly started arriving as Grace and Jilly worked to ensure everything was ready. As they filled their plates and settled at the table, Rebekah came in, a strange expression on her face.

"Um, Grace, Derek is on the front porch. He says if you don't come out immediately, he's going to come in and you won't like what he has to say," Rebekah informed her.

"Oh boy, what does he want now?" Grace asked as she dried her hands and prepared to meet him.

Every time she thought they'd made progress in their contentious relationship, something else happened to ruin it. Since Rebekah had nothing else to say, Grace grabbed her coat and hurried to the porch.

"What can I do for you?" she asked an agitated Derek.

He stopped pacing long enough to hold up a white envelope. "Is this it? Three ghosts, right? You've now given me three cards so we're done? Or is there some grand finale I need to worry about?"

Grace shook her head. "For the last time, I swear I'm not the one sending you those. But yes, there are only three ghosts, so hopefully that's the last card you'll receive."

Derek ran a hand down his face. "I have spent hours racking my brain for someone else, anyone else, that would have a reason to do this, but the only one I can come up with is you. So, please, for the love of all that is holy, stop. You've had your fun, okay? Please stop. That's all I ask."

"Derek, I—"

He shook his head and held up his hand. "I'm going to go now."

Grace watched him leave. She wanted to shout her innocence from the rooftop, but she knew it would fall on deaf ears. So, she did the only thing she could and returned to the kitchen where she found a waiting Rebekah.

"Everything okay?" Rebekah asked.

It wasn't clear if Rebekah was referring to Derek or the text message, but Grace chose to focus on the reason she'd summoned Rebekah in the first place. She pulled her phone out of her pocket, navigated to the picture of the engagement announcement she'd taken last night, then handed the phone to Rebekah.

The color drained from Rebekah's face as her eyes stared at the announcement. Without uttering a single word, she turned on her heel and made a beeline for the stairs in the foyer, Grace following close behind. When she reached the door to her mother's room, she shoved it open without knocking, entered the room, then slammed it shut behind her.

Even though she wanted to witness the confrontation, Grace chose to remain behind in the hallway. That didn't stop her from hovering outside the door so she could eavesdrop.

"So, this is why you're here," Rebekah shouted at Jackie.

Grace pictured in her mind Rebekah shoving the phone in Jackie's face.

"I see that 'friend' of yours can add meddling brat to her list of unappealing character traits," Jackie said in a condescending tone.

That woman never stopped with the insults, did she?

"This has nothing to do with Grace and everything to do with you and Dad," Rebekah replied. "How could you do this? How could you announce an engagement between me and some guy I've only met once?"

"Honestly, Rebekah, you need to calm down. Your father and I know what's best for you, we always have. All you need to do is come home and everything will be as it was meant to be."

Silence deafened the hallway, and Grace suddenly wished she had followed Rebekah in after all.

"You are delusional," Rebekah finally uttered. "Instead of going home with you, I think I need to take you to a doctor since you clearly have some sort of illness."

Sounds of pacing could be heard from the room as Grace prepared to intervene if it became necessary.

"You know what? I think I need to call the family attorney and ask what it would take to have you both committed to the care of a doctor. Yes, that's exactly what I should do."

"Don't waste your time," Jackie replied, through what sounded like gritted teeth. "You know that would never happen."

"Maybe, maybe not, but it would certainly cause quite the scandal, wouldn't it, Mother? I can see it now: 'Rebekah Rutherford Questions Parents' Sanity' splashed all over the society pages. Even if nothing came of it, I highly doubt Thomas, or any other man you manage to scrounge up, would want anything to do with a family name as tainted as ours will be by the time I get through with it."

Grace heard Jackie gasp, and imagined her hand flying to her mouth, or maybe her heart. She couldn't help but grin at the scenario Rebekah painted. It would be her parents' worst nightmare and just might be enough of a threat to get Jackie to voluntarily return to New York.

"I must say, you disappoint me. After everything your father and I have done for you, this is how you repay us—"

"Yeah, yeah," Rebekah interrupted. "Please save your sob story for someone who cares. You put a roof over my head and food on the table, congratulations, you fulfilled the bare-minimum duty as parents. That does not entitle you to my life."

Jackie huffed. "I would hardly call designer clothes, expensive food, private schools, and a penthouse overlooking the park the 'bare minimum.' But I suppose I have only myself to blame for your entitlement. Somewhere along the way, I failed to instill in you proper values."

"And for that, I thank you," Rebekah snarked. "The last thing I want is to share your 'values.' You have two choices: either take the first plane back to New York tomorrow morning, or I start making phone calls. You have until tonight to decide, no exceptions."

"This isn't over," Jackie said quietly.

"It is for me," Rebekah replied sadly. "When I first saw you standing in Grace's foyer, I actually thought that maybe, just maybe, you'd had a change of heart and come to reconcile. I thought, if Amelia Parish can change, maybe my mom could, too. How foolish of me," Rebekah sighed. "You'll never change, will you, Mom?"

Grace jumped back when Rebekah opened the door. "Sorry, I..."

Rebekah shook her head. "It's fine, it saves me from having to relay everything that happened."

"I'm really sorry," Grace said. She threw her arms around Rebekah and pulled her close. Her heart ached for her friend, and her arms tightened further when she felt Rebekah begin to shake.

They remained like that for several minutes, and when Rebekah pulled away, Grace hurried into the bathroom to grab tissue for her to blow her nose.

"Is there anything I can do?" Grace asked softly.

"No, but thanks," Rebekah sniffed. "All we can do now is hope she takes my threats seriously and leaves."

Grace was already praying for that outcome, but she didn't tell Rebekah that. "We're supposed to go choose a Christmas tree for the living room today, want to come with us? Don't forget I promised to hang your handmade ornaments front and center on the tree!"

Rebekah smiled. "I'm supposed to work today, but you know what, I would love to come!"

"Great! It's settled then. One awesome Christmas tree outing coming up!"

"You are such a goofball," Rebekah replied with a laugh.

Grace wrapped her arm around Rebekah's shoulders and led her toward the stairs. "That's why you love me," she sing-songed.

The look on Rebekah's face turned serious. "One of many reasons," Rebekah replied. "Thanks, Grace, I honestly don't know what I'd do without you."

"You'd probably end up on some reality show about housewives," Grace teased.

Rebekah snorted and would have tripped on the stairs had Grace not caught her. "I should be offended by that, but you're probably right. Is there a New York version of that? If there's not, we should sign my mom up!"

"I'll look into it," Grace promised. "For now, let's go have some fun. You're going to love the Christmas tree farm!"

-Five-

G race sat on the couch and admired the Christmas tree. The guests had chosen a gorgeous nine-foot Balsam Fir, and the vivid scent had caused the entire first floor of the house to smell like Christmas. The decorations were a hot mess, with bits of glue and glitter everywhere, but that only added to the charm. And, true to her word, Grace had hung Rebekah's ornaments front and center.

When Jilly appeared in the doorway, Grace turned to greet her with a smile. "You look a little less frazzled this morning!"

"You have no idea," Jilly replied. She made a noise that was somewhere between a sigh and a laugh. "What's on the agenda for today?"

"I'm planning a ski trip," Grace announced enthusiastically. "To be safe, I'd like to bring a lunch for everyone, just in case the resort doesn't have options for my gluten-free people."

Jilly raised her brow in skepticism. "You're planning a ski trip? Around here?"

Grace stood and followed Jilly into the kitchen. "Believe it or not, there's a ski resort up near the north side of

Kansas City. They make their own snow and everything, so no waiting around for Mother Nature to cooperate!"

"Wow, I had no idea. That sounds like so much fun, your guests are going to have a blast!" Jilly exclaimed in excitement.

"That's the plan. Want to come? There's always room for one more."

Jilly began to pull ingredients out of the fridge and set them on the counter. "I would love to, but after I get breakfast and lunch finished, I need to work on dinner, clean the bathrooms, and then pick the kids up from daycare. Plus, I still need to figure out a permanent place to live as well as what I'm going to do for work." She stopped what she was doing and took a deep breath. "I don't know, Grace, things are not looking good."

"Why? Have your in-laws done something else?" Grace asked in concern.

"Not yet," she said with a shake of her head. "But they continue to call and leave harassing messages. I think they're hoping if they threaten me enough I'll give in."

"I'm so sorry, I can't imagine dealing with that on top of everything else," Grace replied. She reached out and gave her friend a quick hug. "On the bright side, I may have a way to help. I don't know if you've heard, but Bea is planning to retire at the end of the month."

After another deep breath, Jilly resumed work, this time grabbing pans out of the cupboard. "I did hear that. Why?"

"I think taking over the bakery would be perfect for you," Grace told her. "Think about it, it would give you the job security you need, plus a schedule that would allow you to be home with the kids in the afternoons and evenings."

"That sounds great, but I can't imagine I have anywhere even close to enough money to buy a business like that. Especially when I still need to find a house, and then furnish that house...I don't know Grace, I think I need to just find an office job."

Grace pursed her lips. This was not going at all like she had planned. "An office job would require you to work nine to five, and I can't help but notice there are very few of those in Winterwood. So, tack on at least an hour to commute each way, the cost of gas and wear and tear on your car, and then ask yourself if it's still worth it."

"When you put it like that, it sounds horrible," Jilly said with a laugh. "But that still doesn't solve my money problems."

"Why don't you talk to Bea and see what happens?" Grace suggested. "It's possible the two of you could work something out."

Jilly began to crack eggs into a hot skillet. "I suppose it wouldn't hurt," she agreed hesitantly.

"Good morning!" Carl called out in a cheerful voice.

Grace and Jilly turned to look in his direction, both of them startled by the interruption.

"Good morning," Grace replied once she'd recovered from the surprise. "You're up early. How did you sleep?"

"I'm always up with the roosters!" Carl joked. "I slept well, though, no complaints. What are we up to today?"

"Skiing!" Grace replied, a huge grin spreading across her face. She quickly launched into the same spiel she'd just given Jilly when she saw the confused look on Carl's face. "So, what do you think?" she asked when she was finished. "Are you ready to hit the slopes?"

Ross and Megan entered the room hand-in-hand. "Did we just hear you mention skiing?"

If only they had come up with this plan before the guests had booked, then Grace wouldn't have to explain over and over again the logistics of skiing in an area without snow. As it was, she relayed the plans for the third time, relieved when her guests showed excitement for her plan.

"That sounds awesome!" Megan exclaimed. She turned toward Ross and wrapped an arm around his waist. "Skiing was our second choice," Megan explained to Grace. "So it's pretty cool we'll still get to do that. It's like we're getting the best of both worlds!"

Ross did not look as convinced, but Grace hoped he would change his mind once they arrived at the resort. She couldn't help but think he must really love his wife if he was willing to give up a ski trip for a stay at a bed and breakfast in a small, Midwestern town. Now Grace really felt the pressure to make sure she provided her guests with an experience to remember.

Once the others arrived, Grace explained the plan for the fourth time. This time, she did her best to hype up the trip with as much enthusiasm as possible. The twins looked excited, Arnie and Teddy looked relieved, likely because the previous day's events had not appealed to them, but Louisa and Hannah exchanged worried glances.

"I don't know," Louisa grimaced. "What would we do with the babies? It's not like they can ski."

"Nor is it safe for us to ski with them," Hannah pointed out.

Leo and Leora's shoulders sagged as they slumped down in their chairs, and Grace was reminded of how miserable they'd looked the day before when Molly, Louisa, and Hannah had spent all their time fawning over the babies and basically ignoring everyone else. Grace, Carl, and Katherine had tried to make it up to them, but Grace had a feeling this was more common than Hannah realized.

"I can watch the babies," Grace volunteered. "That way, you guys can all have fun without worrying about the little ones."

"By yourself?" Louisa asked.

The look on her face suggested she did not believe Grace was up for that particular challenge. "As I'm sure Molly can attest, I have plenty of experience babysitting," Grace said defensively. "They'll probably just sleep most of the time anyway."

"I don't know," Hannah said hesitantly. "No offense, but we've only known you a couple of days. Leaving our babies with a stranger is a lot to ask."

Grace wanted to snap that allowing strangers in her home wasn't much different, but she managed to hold her tongue. She didn't actually care one way or the other; it's not like she was looking forward to spending the day changing diapers. She just wanted to give Leo and Leora a chance to spend some quality time with their parents.

Molly finally decided to chime in. "Grace is amazing with Eliza," she assured them. "I wouldn't hesitate to leave my baby with her. If it would make you more comfortable,

I could work from home today and Grace and I could watch them together."

"If I stay here, who will drive the bus?" Grace asked.

Grant folded the newspaper he'd been reading and set it on the table next to his plate. "I suppose this is where I come in?" He sat up straight and did a little shrug. "I guess I could take a day off."

Teddy high-fived Grant. "That's the spirit! Maybe us boys will have ourselves a little competition."

"What about me?" Leo asked, his frown deepening.

"You too, buddy," Teddy said as he ruffled Leo's short blonde hair.

Some of Leo's earlier excitement finally returned to his face, and suddenly Grace felt all her efforts were worth it.

"Well, then I guess it's settled," Grace announced to the table. "Jilly has prepared lunch for you to take with you, so all that's left for you to do is dress warmly and load onto the bus!"

Louisa and Hannah still seemed hesitant, so Grace sought to reassure them. "We can do a video call any time you want, and Molly, Granny, Gladys, and even Jilly will all be around until you get back."

Hannah smiled. "I'm being ridiculous," she said with a laugh. "I'm sure everything will be fine. Just promise you'll call if something happens."

"I promise," Grace replied. She held her first two fingers up to her forehead in a salute. "Scout's honor."

Thankfully, that seemed to do the trick, and twenty minutes later, the moms loaded the bus with everyone else. Grace watched them drive off, sad she couldn't go but relieved she'd get a break from hosting duties. She then returned to the dining room where all three babies were lined up on the dining room table, each in their car seat.

"What should I do now?" Grace asked Molly.

Molly looked up from her laptop. "I don't know, whatever you want."

"How long do you think the girls will be asleep?"

She looked at her watch. "At least another hour, maybe longer. Why?"

"If it's okay with you, I'd like to run over to the high school and check in with Conor. The play is a big part of our Christmas Experience this year, and since we only have a few days left until Christmas Eve, I just want to make sure everything is on schedule."

"Sounds good to me. If the girls wake up before you get back, I'll just call Gladys and Granny in to help."

Grace nodded and hurried to grab her coat and purse. She didn't love the idea of abandoning her babysitting duties, but knew Molly had things covered. At least until feeding time, and Grace was certain she'd be back by then.

Once she arrived at the high school, she headed toward the gym where the play was to take place, then oohed and aahed when she saw the stage.

"This looks amazing," she said to Conor. "Did you do all this?" she asked as she waved her hand toward the Dickens-themed backdrops.

"I helped, but this is mostly the work of the kids," Conor said, beaming with pride. "They did an amazing job, didn't they?"

"Absolutely!" Grace agreed. "How is everything going? Will you be ready by Christmas Eve?"

Conor nodded. "We plan to do a practice run earlier that day for parents and friends, but if everything goes to plan, we'll be ready."

"Great! Is there anything you need from me?"

"Have you decided on the number of tickets you need yet?"

Grace mentally counted everyone in her head again. "To be safe, I'd like to get thirty. I think I only need twenty-eight or twenty-nine, but it never hurts to have a couple of extra, just in case."

Conor whistled. "That's a lot of tickets!"

"Tell me about it," Grace joked. "These aren't just for guests, they're for friends and family, too."

"Well, I for one appreciate the support, and I know the kids will, too. I've been listening to some of them talk, and while they're nervous to perform for the first time, their biggest fear is no one showing up to watch the play. The thought breaks my heart, so it's a relief to know that's not going to be an issue."

"I would never allow that to happen," Grace assured him. She checked her watch and winced. "I better get back to the house. I'll stop by again in a day or two to pick up the tickets."

Conor walked Grace to the door. "No worries, I'll drop them off on my way home later today."

"Thanks, Conor, I appreciate that. These days I feel like I'm running around like a chicken with its head cut off!" Grace winced again at the image. "Forget I said that."

They both laughed, then Grace returned to her car. On her way home, she realized she hadn't seen Jackie's car when she'd left the house and made a point to look for it when she got home. When it still wasn't there, Grace hurried up to Jackie's room, surprised to see it was empty, all evidence of Jackie gone. She really had left.

Grace called Rebekah.

"What's up?" Rebekah asked when she picked up the phone.

"It looks like your mom left," Grace informed her.

Rebekah made a noise that sounded like a cross between a laugh and a sob. "I guess my threat worked."

"Are you okay?"

"Yeah," Rebekah sighed. "It's what we wanted, right?"

"Not like this," Grace replied.

"No, not like this," Rebekah agreed.

They stood there in silence for a moment before Grace cleared her throat. "Does this mean you'll come back home?"

"Um, yes, but maybe not until the guests leave. This way, you can move into my room so you don't have to sleep on the couch."

These days, Grace actually preferred the couch. With two babies in the house, things were a little noisier than usual and she still hadn't gotten used to that. "Please don't stay away on my account. The couch isn't bad and I don't mind sleeping on it for another few days."

"I'll let you know my plans by the end of the day," Rebekah replied. "Let me know if you need anything in the meantime, okay?"

"Will do." Grace hung up the phone and took one last look around the room, just in case Jackie had simply put her things away instead of vacating. When she still couldn't find evidence of the woman, she breathed a sigh of relief; Jackie was officially gone.

Grace went back downstairs just in time to hear one of the babies begin to cry. She was back on babysitting duty, only six more hours to go until her guests returned. Surely she could handle that?

-Four-

"**A**lright everyone, today's event is," Grace excitedly announced as she began to drum her fingers on the dining table, "a candy crawl!"

Silence echoed throughout the room, followed by all eyes turning to stare at her.

"Um, okay, I really thought you guys would be more excited," Grace said nervously.

"I think everyone's still tired, dear," Granny assured her.

Several heads nodded in agreement.

"I'm surprised I even made it down the stairs," Carl groaned. "I thought I was in good shape, but hours of skiing yesterday proved me wrong."

A chorus of 'mmhmms' and 'me too's' came from around the table.

"We want to do the candy crawl!" Leora said enthusiastically.

"Yeah, we love candy!" Leo agreed.

Great, it looked like Grace would need another backup plan. "How about I set you guys up in the living room with some popcorn and Christmas movies, while I take the kids downtown?"

Hannah yawned as she stretched out her aching arms. "That would be lovely, though I wouldn't mind a morning nap instead."

"If you don't mind, Grace, I think we all might appreciate a little down time this morning. Could we save the movies for this afternoon?" Carl asked. He was already pushing back his chair and standing.

"Of course," Grace assured them. "We will see you all later."

Grace hurried to clear the table while the rest of the adults trudged upstairs. "If you two want to go and grab your coats, I should be ready by the time you get back," she told the twins.

As soon as they were gone, Hannah, who had lagged behind, approached Grace. "I just wanted to say thank you," she said to Grace.

"Oh, you're welcome," Grace replied. "I'm sure the kids will have a great time!"

"I am, too, but that's not why I'm thanking you." Hannah paused for a moment. "Well, actually, I should thank you for that, too. Anyway, what I'm trying to say is, until yesterday I had no idea I was neglecting the twins, but the ski trip, and more importantly, you watching Lexi, made that apparent. Once I had some time away from the baby, I realized just how much I was prioritizing her."

Grace wasn't sure what to say. That had been her intention, but she didn't want to admit that, nor did she want to make the woman feel bad by agreeing. "I'm glad you were able to spend some quality time with the twins," she said cautiously. "I'm sure it's hard trying to juggle parenting a couple of pre-teens along with a newborn."

Hannah's face melted into a smile. "You know, it's really nice that someone gets that, thank you. It's been so long since I had a baby, I'd practically forgotten what it was like. It feels like I'm starting all over again, which, to be fair, I kind of am. But that doesn't excuse my behavior. The twins still need their mother, and from this point forward, I plan to make sure I spend an equal amount of time with them as well."

"I'm sure they will love that," Grace said warmly. Since the conversation seemed to have reached a conclusion, she excused herself to get ready, then made a quick detour into the kitchen. "I'll take care of the dishes as soon as I get back," Grace said to Jilly.

"Don't worry about it," she replied. "If I get a chance, I'll load them into the dishwasher."

Grace paused for a moment. "I really want things to work out for you with Bea and the bakery, but you have no idea how much I'm going to miss you."

Jilly laughed and gave Grace a quick hug. "I'm not going anywhere, silly."

"You just won't be here," Grace sighed. "I don't know what I'm going to do without your help." That was the understatement of the century. Grace's life had become so much better when Jilly had agreed to work for her part-time. More than anything, Grace wished she had enough work to hire her full-time, but with a seasonal business, that just wasn't possible. She would have to find someone else, and in a town this size, that was easier said than done.

Luckily, Leo and Leora chose that moment to burst through the door, effectively putting an end to Grace's pity party.

"We're ready," they yelled out in unison.

Their enthusiasm was infectious and Grace couldn't help but smile back at them. "Alright, let's go!" She said goodbye to Jilly, then led the kids outside and down the street to Bea's Bakery. They had arranged in advance to start there, and Bea was waiting for them with stockings full of cookies and cupcakes to start off the candy crawl.

"Where's everyone else?" Bea asked in bewilderment. She laid the large box full of stockings on a nearby table and allowed the kids to choose their own.

"They're at home resting," Grace explained. "The ski trip wore them out. Well, all except for these two!"

The twins looked up at Bea and grinned. "I won the competition for the most times down the hill!" Leo told her.

"And I won the competition for the fastest time down the hill!" Leora bragged.

"That's only because you fell and tumbled down the hill head-first," Leo retorted. When Leora rolled her eyes, he stuck his tongue out at her.

"It still counts," Leora pouted.

Grace's eyes went wide as she looked at Bea for help.

"Now kids, you can both be winners," Bea assured them. "Are you ready to go to the next store?"

They perked up at the mention of more treats, and Grace mouthed a silent thank you to her friend.

"I'll drop the rest of these off at your place later," Bea told Grace, as she nodded toward the rest of the stockings.

"That would be great, thanks," Grace replied. "We walked down here, otherwise I would take them back with me. We're supposed to do a movie marathon after lunch, so this will be a nice surprise for the others."

"Oh, in that case, I'll whip up some popcorn balls and add them to the stockings," Bea replied.

Grace appreciated her thoughtfulness but knew how busy Bea was. "That would be great, but please don't go out of your way for us. I have some microwave popcorn at home, and can always grab more from the store if needed."

"I'll see what I have time to do," Bea said absentmindedly. Her gaze had drifted to the window and she was now staring at something out on the street.

"What are you looking at?" Grace asked, her curiosity getting the better of her.

Bea turned her attention back to Grace, a guilty look on her face. "I was watching Lyda and Derek," she admitted sheepishly.

Grace moved to look out the window, and sure enough, Lyda and Derek appeared to be deep in conversation across the street. That is, until two boys Grace could only assume were her kids came running up to her. The look of disappointment on Lyda's face mirrored the one on Grace's when Derek quickly excused himself.

"I should go say hi," Grace said out loud. She turned to face Bea and the twins and grimaced. "I don't think my match-making efforts are paying off this time."

"You never know," Bea said with a shrug. "Derek's a tough one, it's going to take some time to break through that shell of his."

Leo and Leora had started to get antsy. "We should get going," Grace said, motioning for the kids to follow. "Bye, Bea, thanks for everything!" Grace called over her shoulder as she led the way outside.

As soon as they were back on the street, Grace made a beeline for Lyda. "Hey," she called out.

Lyda turned toward the sound of Grace's voice and smiled when she saw her. "Hey, yourself," she greeted. "Who do we have here?" she asked, nodding toward the twins.

"This is Leo and Leora," Grace told her. "They're staying at the B&B with us this Christmas. Are those your boys?" Grace asked in return, though given how much they looked like Lyda, it wasn't necessary to ask.

"Yep," she said, putting an arm around each one. "This one is Colton," she said, indicating the older one, "and this one is Weston," she said, nodding to the other one.

"They're a lot older than I thought," Grace said in surprise. The way Lyda had talked about them, she'd been expecting toddlers, not elementary-aged kids.

Lyda chuckled as the boys gave her a funny look.

"We're nine and ten," Colton informed Grace.

"Yeah," Weston chimed in. "We're practically men."

It was hard, but Grace managed not to laugh at the boys' serious tone.

"Can we go to the next store?" Leo asked, his patience wearing thin.

"Of course," Grace said quickly. "Do you guys want to join us?" she asked Lyda.

"We've already been down this side, but we still have the other side to go," Lyda replied. "How about we catch up to you at the end, and then maybe we can take these guys over to the park?"

The kids seemed to love that idea, so Grace agreed, then set off toward the next store. She would have to text Hannah to make sure she was okay with the park detour, but figured she'd be delighted to know her kids were making friends. As they crossed the street a second time, Grace glanced at the hotel and felt a pang of guilt over not participating in the candy crawl, but did her best to shove those feelings aside. She couldn't do everything, so no need to feel guilty every time an opportunity came up she had to decline.

They stopped by a hair salon, a tax prep office, the VFW, and a realtor's office, before going inside Wilkin's Five and Dime. Mr. Wilkins was in his usual jovial mood and happily handed out flavored candy canes, as well as Christmas-themed stickers Grace prayed would not end up on her walls or furniture. After that was Chrissy's boutique, who handed out chocolate Santas, an insurance company who gave each kid one mini Tootsie Roll, and then a pizza parlor that was handing out mini pizza bites, which, much to the kids' chagrin, Grace had to politely decline due to their gluten allergy.

That last one almost caused a meltdown, but once Grace promised they could make their own pizza at home, the crisis was averted. At that point, it was time to cross back over to the other side of the street where they hit up an antique store, a church, and then a bank, before they arrived at the soon-to-be new coffee shop, where a woman was standing outside handing out large candy-cane-shaped containers full of different kinds of candy.

"You must be Brynn," Grace said, recognizing the woman from the town hall meeting.

"Yes, and you're...Grace?" she replied hopefully.

Grace nodded and smiled. "It's nice to finally meet you. We've been waiting for your shop to open so we could come and officially introduce ourselves. Myself and my friends and family," Grace added when she saw the confused look on the woman's face.

Brynn smiled as she let the kids choose a candy cane. "I'm getting there, but there's still so much to do," she replied. "I had no idea how much effort it would take to get this shop up and going before I started, but I'm too invested now to quit, so on I go!"

"Is there anything I can do to help?" Grace asked, even though the last thing she had time for was another project.

"No, but thank you," Brynn replied. "All that's left is a bunch of little decisions that seem to add up, you know what I mean?"

Yes, Grace absolutely did know what she meant. She wanted to continue the conversation but knew the kids were getting restless again, so she would have to stop by another time when things were less hectic. "I'll see you around," Grace said, feeling rather lame at her abrupt exit.

"Yep, stop by anytime," Brynn called out.

By the time they reached the end of the street, Lyda and the boys were waiting for them. The four kids took off running ahead, while Lyda and Grace trailed after them.

"What I wouldn't give to have that amount of energy again," Lyda said wistfully.

"Me, too," Grace agreed, though she wasn't sure she ever had that amount of energy. "I saw you talking to Derek, how did that go?"

Lyda groaned. "It was going well until he saw the kids. But that was to be expected."

"He was probably just surprised," Grace said thoughtfully. "That, or he had somewhere to be. He is a pretty busy man."

"Maybe," Lyda said reluctantly.

"It's also possible when he saw the kids, he assumed you were married," Grace pointed out.

A bitter look flashed across Lyda's face before she shook it off and her smile returned. "He would be wrong, if that's what he thought."

Grace wanted so badly to ask about Lyda's ex, she had to bite her lip to keep the words from spilling out.

"We're divorced," Lyda said with a dry laugh. When Grace looked at her in surprise, she laughed again. "I could tell by the look on your face you were dying to ask."

"I'm sorry," Grace said, shame washing over her at her nosiness. "I'm not a fan of gossip, yet I can't seem to help being nosy."

"As long as you don't go running off to tell the world, it's fine," Lyda replied. "The short version is, we married too young. He joined the army right out of high school and we married right before he left for basic training. At first, things were great, but I think that was only because he wasn't around enough for us to fight. He was stationed several times in areas where family wasn't allowed to go, but then he received orders to spend three years in a country where the family could go, only he still didn't want us to come. It was at that point I realized it was over. So, we divorced and here I am, trying to start over back in the town where it all began."

Lyda's face maintained its smile, but her tone belied her feelings of bitterness and anger. Grace felt awful for her friend, and even worse for wanting her to relive such painful memories. "I'm really sorry," Grace said lamely. She wished there was something else to say, because 'I'm sorry' just wasn't enough.

"Don't feel bad for me," Lyda replied. "I made my choices and I paid for them, fair and square. I would say I regret them, and to an extent I do, but I will never regret my boys so..."

Grace gave her a side hug, then let go and resumed speed walking. The kids were now so far ahead, they would have to run to catch them, but Lyda didn't seem concerned. Grace could only hope that meant her kids knew how to get to the park since Leo and Leora did not. Maybe she wasn't such a good babysitter after all.

A few more moments passed before Grace felt capable of responding to Lyda's heartbreak. "Your ex was a fool to treat you the way he did, but that doesn't mean all men are like that. There is someone out there for you, whether or not that someone is Derek remains to be seen, but I for one, am not giving up."

Lyda laughed, a real laugh this time, and bumped Grace's shoulder with her own. "You're just saying that because you're in love, silly!"

"Why do you say that?" Grace asked in confusion.

"Oh come on, everyone knows that when someone's in love they want everyone else to be in love, too. But don't worry about me, okay? I'm happy with my life the way it is. If someone happens to come along that fits in with me and the boys, great, if not, well, that's okay, too."

Grace didn't quite believe her, but she wasn't going to argue. There was plenty of time to play matchmaker. For now, she had kids and a house full of guests to worry about. She would just have to take things one problem at a time.

-Three-

T he big day had finally arrived—well, one of the big days—it was time for the Christmas Festival and tree-lighting ceremony! It was also the one day Grace had to depend on Derek. The same Derek who believed she was 'haunting' him and was currently avoiding her calls. She'd tried to check in with him multiple times to make sure he would be at the ceremony that night, but each call went directly to voicemail. Had he blocked her number? She didn't know, but she wouldn't be surprised if he had.

Her guests were so excited for the festival, they'd finished breakfast in record time and were now assembling in the foyer so Grace could lead them over to the park. Since Leo and Leora had been there yesterday, they'd spent the evening regaling the adults with tales of all the booths and decorations they'd seen. Grace was a little concerned they might have hyped the festival up a little too much, but hoped the adults were simply playing along with the excitement for the kids' sake.

"Is everyone ready to go?" Grace asked the group.

"Yes!" the group cheered.

Grace laughed. "Okay then, let's go!" She led the way out of the house, pausing long enough for the moms to get their baby strollers down the stairs. Once that was done, she took off as fast as she dared, considering the mix of elderly, young, and thirty-somethings she was leading. To her surprise, the elderly were soon passing her.

As they raced past, Grace fell back to join the other women.

"The babies are so cute in their little winter outfits," Megan gushed.

Hannah and Louisa exchanged a look.

"Looks like it won't be long before you're in the club," Hannah teased.

Megan looked at her in surprise. "It would be fun to have a baby by next Christmas, but Ross and I have decided to wait a few years."

"That's what Arnie and I said, too, yet here we are," Louisa said as she waved her hand toward Rosalyn.

Grace had no desire to be a part of this conversation, so she hurried to catch up with Carl and Katherine.

"You two seem to have recovered from the ski trip," Grace teased them.

"We don't stay down for long," Carl winked. "Katherine and I have been talking about buying a camper and traveling around the country. There are a lot of places we'd love to visit before we go."

It was obvious what he meant by 'go,' but Grace wasn't ready to think about that, so she chose to focus on the camper. "That sounds awesome! Where would you go first?"

"I've always wanted to go to Yellowstone National Park," Katherine replied. "Geographically speaking, that's probably a silly place to start, given we live in Louisiana, but I would like to work my way there."

Carl nodded. "I wouldn't mind traveling around to all the national parks. Of course, we'll probably need a second camper just to hold all of Katherine's souvenirs!"

Katherine laughed and playfully swatted at his arm. "Says the guy sleeping in his childhood bed," she teased.

Grace laughed with them, then, since they'd reached the park, she waited for everyone to catch up and gather in a circle.

"Okay, everyone, there are food trucks, game booths, craft booths, and fire pits for you to hang out at when you need to warm up. You are free to travel back and forth between here and the house if you need a break, a nap, or are just done for the day. The parade will take place around six and will end with the tree-lighting ceremony in the middle of the park. Lunch and dinner will be available at the house for those of you who want it. Any questions?"

"Where will you be, in case we need you?" Hannah asked.

"I will be either here or at the house," Grace informed them. "I will have my phone on at all times, so if you can't find me, feel free to call."

"Anyone else have a question?" Grace asked. When no one spoke up, she continued. "Awesome, have fun, and like I said, if you need me, just call."

Once the group had dispersed, Grace looked around and spotted Megan and Ross off to the side. She was about to ask them if they needed anything when she saw Ross stomp off in the direction of the house.

"Is everything okay?" Grace asked a visibly upset Megan.

Megan quickly swiped at her eyes and nodded. "Yep, just a little misunderstanding," she said as she pasted on a smile.

It was clear that wasn't quite true, but Grace didn't want to pry, so she chose to distract Megan instead. "There's a booth I would love to show you," Grace said as she began to walk in the direction of the colorful tents. "One of the ladies in town knits scarves, and she has them on display."

"Ooh, I love scarves!" Megan replied as her hand went to the colorful scarf currently wrapped around her neck.

Her reaction was exactly what Grace had hoped for. They had almost reached the tent when Grace saw a flash of movement out of the corner of her eye. As she turned to see what it was, she spotted Jackie, dressed as if she'd just stepped off the runway at Paris Fashion Week—Winter Sports Edition—an equally well-dressed man on her arm.

"Uh oh," Grace muttered. "It looks like there's about to be some fireworks."

Megan looked at Grace in confusion. "Isn't it a little early for that?"

"Not those kind of fireworks," Grace replied as she watched Jackie march across the grass and head straight for Rebekah and Thorne, who happened to be deep in conversation at one of the fire pits. "Excuse me," Grace said to Megan. If she was quick, she might be able to get to Jackie before she reached Rebekah.

"What do you think you're doing?" Jackie huffed as Grace grabbed her arm and steered her in another direction.

"I'm preventing you from causing a scene in front of all these people," Grace explained.

Jackie planted her feet and refused to move another inch. "I can just as easily cause a scene from here, you know."

"Yes, but that will only give Rebekah ammunition to use against you in your medical evaluation," Grace reminded her. "You may have forgotten about that, but I highly doubt Rebekah has."

"You should be ashamed of yourselves, threatening an older woman like that," Jackie admonished. "Mental health is not a joke."

"No, it isn't," Grace agreed. "But it's very difficult to believe that a woman in her right mind would arrange an engagement between her daughter and a stranger without the daughter's knowledge."

The man, who up to this point had remained silent, raised a brow. "What do you mean Rebekah doesn't know?" he asked Jackie. "I thought you told me Rebekah was on board?"

Jackie gave Grace a disgusted look. "Do you see what you've done? Your meddling is ruining everything."

Grace burst out laughing. She couldn't help it; the situation was too absurd to warrant anything else. "You can't be serious," she wheezed. "What did you think would happen when you confronted Rebekah? That she would take one look at Mr. Heartthrob over here and then launch herself into his waiting arms?" She turned to the man. "No offense," she told him. "I'm sure you're perfectly lovely."

He grinned at Grace. "No offense taken."

"Look, I can't stop you from carrying out whatever crazy plan this is supposed to be, but if you continue, you are going to make a fool of yourself. And if you do it here, the whole town is going to bear witness to it. Are you sure that's what you want?" Grace asked Jackie, as she hoped to appeal to her pride and vanity.

"No, that's not what she wants," Rebekah said from behind Jackie.

They all turned to stare at Rebekah, who was standing with her arms crossed and a look of sheer hostility on her face. "I can't believe this," she spat. "I thought you went home, but no, here you are again, ready for round two of 'how fast can I destroy my daughter's life.'"

"What life?" Jackie asked. She lifted her sunglasses and gave Rebekah an appraising once-over. "I don't know what this is," she said as she waved her hand over Rebekah's outfit, "but it is not the life of someone of your station."

"My station?" Rebekah drawled, her nose crinkling in disgust. "What is this, the eighteen hundreds?"

Jackie looked around, her nose lifting in the air. "That's what it looks like to me."

Rebekah rolled her eyes. "Go home, seriously. There is nothing you can say or do that is going to cause me to change my mind. So please, just go home." She shook her head sadly and walked back to Thorne, who was waiting for her by the fire pit. When she reached him, he pulled her into his arms and sent Jackie a look that would have reduced a lesser woman to a puddle.

"Well, I feel like that settles that," Grace said cheerfully. "Do you need help getting to the airport? I can call you a taxi? Or heck, I'll even take you myself."

"This isn't over until I say it's over," Jackie warned. "Come along, Tom. We can deal with this another time."

Tom shrugged and gave a little half-wave before following after Jackie.

Grace watched them leave, then checked her watch. It was almost time for lunch, which meant it was time for her to run by the house and make sure everything was ready for those who chose to eat at home. When she finally made it back to the dining room, she saw that Jilly had already set everything out and made a mental note to remind her friend of how grateful she was to her.

As she finished pouring a drink, Ross entered the dining room. "Hey," she said cautiously. "Lunch is ready if you're hungry."

Ross nodded but kept his gaze averted.

She knew she shouldn't pry, but her guest's happiness was important to her, so she did it anyway. "Is everything okay?" she asked gently.

He sighed and ran a hand through his hair. "It's fine," he said warily. "It's just, you know, marriage is hard sometimes."

Since she wasn't married yet, she wasn't sure she did know, but chose not to split hairs. Relationships, of all kinds, were hard sometimes. "I understand," she replied. "If you want to talk about it, I'm a good listener."

"Did Megan put you up to this?" he asked suspiciously.

"No," Grace shook her head. "I haven't talked to Megan. I just happened to see you here and thought I would offer a friendly ear if you needed one."

Ross grabbed a bowl and began to ladle beef stew into it. "I know this is going to sound bad, but I feel like my marriage is one-sided. Like, we agree on things, and then Megan just changes things without asking."

"I'm assuming you're referring to this trip?" Grace asked him. They sat down across from each other at the table.

"Yeah, exactly. We had agreed on a ski trip to Colorado, and then, at the last minute, she decides she wants to come here instead."

"So, she changed your plans without telling you?" Grace asked in disbelief.

He shook his head. "No, she told me."

"Okayyy," Grace drawled. "I'm not sure I understand."

"She told me she wanted to come here, so I said fine in order to avoid a fight. But she should have known I wouldn't be happy about ditching my friends for some lame trip to the middle of nowhere." Ross winced. "No offense."

Grace chose to ignore that and focus on the real issue. "Why did you assume that telling Megan you would rather stick to your original plans would cause a fight?"

"I don't know, because," he said lamely. "Megan's family was really big on traditions while she was growing up, and now that she's lost her parents, it's important to her to keep those traditions alive." He paused and looked down at his soup bowl. "I sound like a jerk, don't I?"

"You sound like someone who's trying to navigate the fragile lines between what you want and what your partner wants," Grace said compassionately. "It's okay to want to go skiing in Colorado, just as it's okay for Megan to want to carry on her family traditions."

"But we can't do both," he pointed out. "So how do we decide which one to do without one of us getting upset?"

Wasn't that the million-dollar question? "Compromise when you can, and then prioritize when you can't," Grace stated.

"That sounds simple, and yet, it really isn't."

"No, but sometimes the best we can do is all we're capable of doing. What really matters here is your ability to communicate. You can't assume Megan knows what you're thinking and feeling. You have to tell her, just as you would want her to tell you."

"You're right," he agreed. "I would be extremely upset if the situations were reversed." He pushed his chair back and stood. "Thanks, Grace. I think I need to go find my wife and apologize."

Grace smiled up at him. "I'm happy I was able to help." She sat for a moment and considered what she'd told Ross. What were people supposed to do when compromise wasn't an option? Or when one could argue that both sides deserved priority? She wished she had the answer to that. She was about to get up when a pair of hands covered her eyes.

"Guess who," Cole whispered in her ear.

"Hey," she said as she reached back to hug him. "What are you doing here?"

He pulled her out of the chair and into his arms. "I've been looking for you," he replied. "Carl said he thought you might be here."

She hugged him tighter, grateful for the opportunity to spend time with him. "I was about to take Granny and Gladys some lunch. Do you want to join me?"

"I would love to," he smiled down at her. "But first..." he trailed off as he leaned down to meet her lips with his. When he finished, he leaned back and traced the side of her face with his fingertips. "I miss you," he said softly.

"I miss you, too," she whispered back. "Have there been any more mishaps with Piper and the tree?"

Cole groaned. "Let's not talk about that."

Grace laughed. "That bad, huh?" She laughed again as she moved to the kitchen and pulled out a serving tray. "Hopefully next year won't be as bad."

"I have to survive this year first," Cole deadpanned. He grabbed a bowl and began to ladle stew, while Grace loaded the tray with spoons and napkins.

"How about I come over later and give Piper another stern talking to?" Grace asked innocently.

Cole stopped what he was doing and gave her a look. "I think that's a good idea. And while you're there, maybe I can get you to help me with a couple of other things, too?"

"I would be happy to," Grace drawled. She was already counting down the minutes until she could see him again. But for now, she would enjoy the time they had together with Granny and Gladys.

Once the tray was fully loaded, Grace followed Cole into Granny's room. It had felt like an eternity had passed since she'd spent quality time with Granny as well, and it was nice to see her while she could. Every moment with loved ones was an opportunity to create a memory she could cherish, and she planned to do just that.

-Two-

F ourteen hours had passed since the tree lighting ceremony, and Grace was still fuming. Derek had one job, and he still managed to screw that up. Or, more accurately, he chose to screw her over by no-showing the entire event. No warning, no excuse, nothing. And no amount of phone calls brought her any closure either; they still went straight to voicemail.

"You know, dear, it's possible something happened to Derek," Katherine pointed out. "That would also explain why he isn't answering your calls."

Grace didn't want to consider that as an option. No matter how much she currently disliked him, she would never wish harm on the man. It was much better to assume he was just being his usual jerk self than to think he was hurt or worse.

Carl shifted in his chair. "I don't know why you're so upset anyway. The tree lighting ceremony went off without a hitch. I dare say most people weren't the wiser that someone other than you was supposed to lead it."

She stopped pacing long enough to face Carl. "It's the principle of the matter," Grace explained. She looked around Carl and Katherine's cozy room and smiled. At least they were happy. And they were right, none of the other guests knew anything was wrong, still...

"I think you're just upset because this delayed your plans with that young man of yours," Katherine mused.

Was she really that obvious? Yes, yes she was. Since she'd been forced to fill in for Derek, Grace had lost an entire hour with Cole the night before. That might not seem like a big deal, but when you consider how little time they already had together, the molehill became a mountain real quick.

"You're right," Grace admitted. She blew her breath out, lifting the strands of stray hair that had come loose from her ponytail. "I'm sorry. I shouldn't be venting to you guys."

Katherine waved her hand dismissively. "No need to apologize. We're happy to listen any time you need us to. I just don't like seeing you worked up over nothing."

Nor should she be getting worked up over nothing. The stress of the last few days must be getting to her more than she realized. "Thank you. I'm going to choose to calm down now. We're going to have a gingerbread contest if you guys are up for it?"

"That sounds perfect!" Carl exclaimed. "I do believe us old folks won last year. Time for us to claim victory once more!"

Grace and Katherine chuckled.

"I need to go and get everything set up," Grace informed them. "I'm not sure how to divide the teams up this year since we only have two kids. Do you think it would be okay to invite a couple more kids? Or should we divide the teams in a different way?"

Carl appeared to consider that. "So, there are four of us oldies, six of the younger folk, seven counting you, Grace, and then two kids?"

Grace did a mental head count and nodded. "That sounds right. Unless Molly and Grant come, in which case there will be nine people around my age."

"There's also Rebekah," Katherine pointed out. "Which brings us up to ten."

"I don't think I would count on her," Grace replied. "I haven't seen her since the incident with her mother yesterday, and I'm kind of concerned I may not see her again for several days, if then."

Katherine and Carl exchanged a knowing look.

"We're sorry to hear that," Katherine said, her voice full of compassion. "I do not agree at all with what her parents are doing."

Grace plopped down on the edge of the fireplace and rested her chin on her hands. "I just don't get it, is Jackie's behavior normal? It seems so...I don't know, archaic."

"It's a bit over the top," Carl agreed. "But not completely surprising. My parents did something similar with each of us."

"Really?" Grace's brows shot up in surprise. "I know you said last year they had someone they expected you to marry, but I didn't know they went to the extremes Rebekah's parents are going."

Carl shifted again and took a sip of tea. "You have to remember, we aren't talking about a life insurance policy or a couple of stocks and bonds. We're talking about an empire."

Katherine nodded. "Rebekah comes from old money. Her family has businesses and assets to pass down, not just a bank account with some zeroes. They want to ensure that when they pass on, their legacy remains intact with the next generation."

"Why can't Rebekah just inherit the legacy? Why does she need some man?" Grace demanded. It all seemed so unfair. Not only was Rebekah not good enough to inherit on her own, she apparently couldn't even choose the man she wanted to spend her life with.

"I think it's more of an issue of obedience," Katherine explained. "For most of her life, Rebekah fell in line. Now that she's rebelled, her parents no longer feel they can trust her to run the family as they have done. Plus, they're looking for a certain kind of man to welcome into the family."

Ah, Grace was finally beginning to understand. "You mean, a man who thinks like they do?"

"Exactly," Carl nodded in agreement.

"Poor Rebekah," Grace said sadly. "All she wanted was for her parents to love her."

Carl reached over and squeezed Katherine's hand. "While I hope it doesn't take decades for her family to make amends, just remember that you have given her the family she craves. Continue to support her, and she'll be fine."

Grace stood and gave them each a hug. "Thank you, that means a lot to me. Now, I need to go downstairs and get ready." She walked to the door and then turned back. "I just realized we never settled on a way to divide everyone into groups."

"How about you invite the friends for the twins, and then we can split the younger adults into groups of two?" Carl proposed.

"I think that should work," Grace replied. She did the math one more time, and then gave up. She would have to try again once she knew exactly how many people would be participating.

Back in the hallway, Grace sent a quick text to Lyda inviting her and the boys over for the competition. She then tried to call Derek one more time before shoving her phone in her pocket in frustration. As she made her way downstairs, her phone rang, and she pulled it back out of her pocket to see who it was. When she saw Derek's name on the screen, she stepped out onto the porch and hit answer.

"Where have you been? I've been calling you for days," Grace accused.

"I can see that, and I really don't appreciate you blowing up my phone."

Grace stuck her tongue out at the screen, even though he couldn't see it. "I wouldn't have had to blow up your phone if you hadn't ghosted me," she shot back.

"There you are with the ghost comments again," he groaned. "You just can't resist, can you."

They'd been on the phone less than a minute, and Grace already wanted to strangle him. "Can you just explain why you failed to show up to the tree lighting ceremony last night?" she asked through gritted teeth.

There was silence on his end for so long, Grace checked to see if he'd hung up on her.

"I was busy," he finally replied. "It wasn't that big of a deal, so I figured you'd get someone else to cover for me."

"And you didn't think it was necessary to give me a heads up?" she accused.

"I suppose I should have done that," he admitted reluctantly. "But in my defense, I really was busy." He took a deep breath. "Anyway, can you please stop with the barrage of phone calls?"

It was tempting to call him anyway, just to annoy him, but that would be petty, and no matter how much she wanted to, she did not have time for petty. "Fine, whatever," Grace replied. She then hung up without saying goodbye. "Ugh!" she shouted.

"Is this a bad time?" Lyda called out.

Grace turned to see Lyda and the boys coming up the walkway. "Sorry," Grace said, her cheeks turning red from embarrassment. "Please come in. The rest of the group should be waiting for us in the dining room."

"I hope that wasn't the future Mr. Grace Parker," Lyda joked as she passed by Grace on her way into the house.

"No, just my favorite interim mayor," Grace grumbled.

Lyda stopped in the foyer to take off her coat and hang it on the coat rack. "I'm starting to think I may have dodged a bullet, given the way the two of you fight," she mused.

"No," Grace shook her head. "Please don't judge him over that alone. Some people just get along like oil and water. He's not a bad guy, he's just not a fan of me!" Grace chuckled as she finished her thought.

"You are way too kind," Lyda replied as she followed Grace into the dining room.

As expected, the whole crew had assembled at the table and was talking amongst themselves while they waited patiently for Grace to start the competition. She did another headcount and still came up short by two in order to have an equal number of people on each team. It probably wasn't necessary to be this strict, but she didn't want anyone to feel like things were unfair. So, she pulled out her phone and asked Rebekah and Thorne to come and join the fun, and was relieved when they immediately agreed.

While she waited on them, she divided everyone into groups of four: Leo, Leora, Colton, and Weston were on the kids team. Granny, Gladys, Carl, and Katherine were on the old folks team—their words! Arnie, Teddy, Ross, and Grant were on the men's team. Louisa, Hannah, Lyda, and Molly were on the moms' team. And Grace, Megan, Rebekah, and Thorne were on the young and fun team!

"I'm not sure I appreciate the insinuation that I am neither young nor fun, now that I'm a mom," Molly teased.

"Nah, don't worry about that," Hannah chimed in. "They'll be one of us soon enough!"

Grace and Megan both laughed uncomfortably.

Thankfully, Thorne and Rebekah arrived before the conversation continued on along that track, and the competition began in earnest.

"There are multiple categories you could possibly win," Grace said as she passed out gingerbread kits to the various groups. "Fastest build, best decorations, most creative design, best use of candy, and since this is a Traditional Christmas Experience, most traditional design!"

"So, technically, we could each win?" Ross asked.

"Technically," Grace replied. "But we will be voting for the best gingerbread house in each category, so technically, one house could win all five awards."

The kids erupted into cheers as the adults ribbed each other good-naturedly.

"If we're ready, the time starts now," Grace said as she started a timer.

Each group moved to their little corner of the table and began to make plans as they talked quietly so as not to be overheard by the competition. To make sure there was enough room, Grace and her group moved to the breakfast bar.

"What should we do?" asked Rebekah as she toyed with a piece of gingerbread.

"I would love to do a traditional design," Megan said as she looked over her shoulder at the other groups. "I have a feeling we won't have much competition in that category."

Rebekah nodded as she, too, eyed the others. "I bet she's right. The kids will go for the fastest, the older folks will go for the best decorations, the men will go for the candy, and the moms will likely go for the most creative."

That sounded right to Grace as well, so she agreed. "Thorne, are you good with that?"

"Sounds good to me," he said with a shrug. "I've never done this before, so just let me know what to do and I'll try my best."

They set to work, and sure enough, thirty minutes later the kids yelled out they were finished. Since the adults weren't anywhere close to done, they declared them the winner of the fastest time and went back to work. Since they were now bored, the kids went outside to run around while the rest of them meticulously worked on their masterpieces.

Another hour passed before they began to put the finishing touches on the houses. By that point, the kids were in the living room playing a board game and eating snacks.

Once everyone had finished, Grace handed out slips of paper and pens, and told everyone to place their votes. She then gathered them all up and tallied the votes.

"Is everyone ready?" she asked the group. When they all shouted 'yes!', Grace continued. "The winner for the best decoration is: the silver seniors!" Everyone clapped as Granny, Gladys, Katherine, and Carl took a bow. "The silver surfers also won for the best use of candy!"

"Ah man," Arnie said in mock disappointment. "I was sure we had that in the bag."

The group laughed as Louisa gave him a hug. "You're still a winner in my eyes, babe!"

"The winner for the most creative design goes to: the moms!" Grace said as they all took a bow. "Which leaves the most traditional design." Grace quickly tallied the votes for that one. "We won!" she said with a laugh to Megan, Rebekah, and Thorne.

"Everyone won but us," Teddy informed the other men. "We got robbed!"

Grace went to the pantry and pulled out the box full of prizes she'd stored there earlier. "I'm sure your wives will be happy to share their goody bags," Grace told them as she handed out the bags of gourmet candy and cookies.

"Speak for yourself," said Hannah as she playfully swatted Teddy's hand away from her bag.

"What happened to what's yours is mine?" he teased.

"I think you mean, what's yours is mine," she teased back.

As the group continued to joke around, Grace began to pull out items to make sub sandwiches for lunch, with special gluten-free buns for the kids. She looked around the room and smiled; this was what the holidays were about, and she was loving every minute of it.

-One-

I t was time for the breakfast with Santa event, and this year, Grace was prepared. There would be no last-minute cries for help, or rallying of troops. No panic, and no stress, just lots of chaos-free fun! Oh, who was she kidding—chaos seemed to follow her wherever she went, and today was no exception. Jenny, Bea's long-time assistant, had gone AWOL, likely due to her anger at Bea choosing not to sell the bakery to her. Junior, who was supposed to play Santa, had gotten the dates mixed up and was now unavailable, and baby Eliza had a cold, so Grant and Molly were home with her. That left Grace manning the pancakes, Carl in the Santa suit, and Rebekah collecting tickets at the door. It was going to be a long morning.

As Grace flipped pancakes, Carl popped into the kitchen in full Santa regalia.

"What do you think, am I convincing?" he asked as he did a little twirl.

Grace laughed, his enthusiasm infectious. "I bet even the twins will believe you're Santa!"

Carl nodded in satisfaction. "Perfect! I spent extra time on appearance just for them. How are you doing in here? I'm sure Katherine would be happy to help, all you have to do is ask."

That might be true, but Grace couldn't bring herself to do it. She knew Carl would have a blast playing Santa, so she didn't mind asking him to step in, but asking her guest to sweat over a hot stove all morning was a bridge too far. "I think I'll be fine," Grace lied, "but thank you for the offer!"

"Okay," Carl said hesitantly, "but if you change your mind, she should be here soon."

She would absolutely NOT be changing her mind, but she did appreciate how quick her guests were to offer to help, despite the fact they'd paid quite a bit of money to be there. Molly was selective in the people she chose for the B&B, but Grace was still surprised by how truly kind and wonderful the guests always were. She was blessed, and she knew it.

Once Carl had left to take his seat in Santa's chair, Rebekah popped her head in.

"Everything okay in here?" she asked in concern. "I have a couple of minutes before I need to get back out there if you have something I can do quickly."

"I'm fine," Grace replied. "I have a rhythm down and I'm scared to mess it up. How are things out there? How long is the line?"

Rebekah peeked through the door, then turned back to Grace. "You don't want to know."

"Perfect," Grace nodded. "How have things been with you? Any sign of your mom?"

"No, and I'm not sure if I should be thankful or terrified," Rebekah said dryly. "I've never seen my mom this committed to something since that time she was determined to get a refund because her shrimp platter only had five shrimp instead of six."

Grace paused what she was doing to gape at Rebekah. "Are you serious?"

"Unfortunately," she said with a sigh. "In her defense, she did pay a lot of money for that platter." She took another peek out the door. "Looks like I better get back out there. Good luck in here!"

Good luck indeed, she thought as she went back to flipping pancakes.

Moments later, Derek came flying through the door. "What is going on here?" he demanded. "There's a line halfway up the street."

"I really hope you're exaggerating," Grace drawled. "But even if you're not, as you can see, I'm the only one back here. So, either grab an apron and get to work, or get out of here and stop distracting me."

"Honestly," he huffed as he grabbed an apron off the hook near the door. "I can't believe you actually manage to run a business. Every time I turn around, there's something else going on with you."

"Why do I suddenly feel like Bob Cratchit?" Grace asked out loud. She smiled when she heard him suck in a breath. No, she shouldn't be antagonizing him, but boy did he make it difficult not to.

"Just tell me what to do," he snapped.

Grace pointed him toward the pans of sausage. "If you can focus on the sausage, I'll keep making pancakes."

They worked in silence until Grace heard a commotion out in the main room. "I wonder what that's about?"

Derek sighed but put his spatula down and looked through the window in the door. "If you must know, that friend of yours is arguing with an old woman and a man who appears to be around our age."

"Oh no!" Grace exclaimed. "I need to get out there and help!" She moved to exit the kitchen, but Derek stopped her.

"You need to do no such thing," he replied. "Your friend is a big girl, she can handle whatever that nonsense is about. You, on the other hand, need to keep making pancakes."

Grace bristled at being told what to do, especially by Derek, of all people, but she knew he was right. Her presence would not only make things worse for Rebekah, it would further delay moving people through the line. Man, did she hate when he was right. So, she did the mature thing and stuck her tongue out at him, then went back to work.

The silence between them was deafening, so Grace decided to break the ice. "Why do you hate Christmas?"

Derek paused and looked up at the ceiling. "Why do you care?" he asked in exasperation.

Why did she care? It wasn't her business, and they definitely weren't friends, yet she couldn't help but feel sorry for him. There had to be a reason why someone would hate the most magical time of the year, and she was willing to bet it wasn't a good one. "Because I want to understand," she finally replied. It was a lame answer, but it was the best she could come up with.

"So, what, is this the point where I'm supposed to spill my guts and we have some sort of 'heart-to-heart'?" he snarked.

"Whatever," Grace rolled her eyes in annoyance. "You're impossible, you know that?"

"I feel the same way about you," he replied.

There were some people she just could not get through to, and Derek was one of them. It was difficult, but she would have to accept it. When they'd finally served the last patron, Derek took off his apron, put it back on the hook by the door, and then left without so much as a goodbye.

Grace watched him go in stunned silence. Despite their differences, she had done nothing to deserve such a blatant display of rudeness. Mayor Allen could not come back soon enough.

***

"So, let's hear it," Gladys said to the group at the table. "Give us all the juicy gossip!"

Gladys, Granny, Carl, Katherine, Rebekah, and Grace all sat around the dining room table drinking tea and eating Christmas cookies. The rest of the guests had opted to spend the day in the city doing some last-minute shopping and sightseeing. Grace would have rather had a root canal than brave the crowds, but maybe it was different when you were on vacation in a new city? She didn't think so, but she'd never been on a vacation, so what did she know?

"The kids just adored Carl as Santa!" Katherine told the group. "It was the cutest thing ever watching him interact with them."

Carl's cheeks turned red. "I'll admit I had a wonderful time, myself."

"Did any of the kids recognize you?" Granny asked.

He shook his head. "I think Leora might have suspected, but if she did, she played along. As for the rest of the kids, I don't think any of them have seen me long enough to recognize me."

"I'm sorry I missed it," Grace said, placing her hand on his arm. "I would have loved to see you with all the kids!"

Gladys leaned toward Rebekah and cleared her throat. "What's this I heard about you causing a scene?"

Ah, now the inquisition made sense. Gladys had heard about the altercation and wanted the gossip first-hand. Grace hated how quickly news like that spread through the town, but she did her best to ignore it—something that was quite difficult to do when it was happening at her own dining room table.

It was Rebekah's turn for her cheeks to redden. "My mother showed up again with Tom, my alleged fiancé," she explained. "I just cannot seem to get it through her head that I will not be returning to New York, and I will absolutely not be marrying Tom." She shook her head and sighed. "I may have to get a restraining order at the rate she's going."

Gladys clucked her tongue. "Let me know if it truly comes to that. I know a guy who can help."

"Thank you," Rebekah replied. "Though I hope it doesn't."

Granny eyed Grace. "I heard you were cooped up in the kitchen with Derek. How did that go?"

"About as well as one would expect," Grace said, with disgust dripping from every word. "I don't know what his problem is."

Gladys exchanged a glance with Granny. "I've done some more digging, and from what I've learned, it's a really sad story."

A small part of Grace wanted to yell 'I told you so'—though to who, she wasn't sure. All she knew was that she felt vindicated after her earlier musings. But that wasn't very nice, either. So, she did her best to rein in her emotions and prompted Gladys to continue. "What happened?"

"Well, it's like this: Derek has had a lot of bad things happen around Christmas time." She paused to take a sip of tea. "First, his parents announced their divorce right before the holiday when he was in his senior year of high school. Why they did that, I will never understand. It would not have killed them to wait and tell him at another time, but who knows what goes through the minds of others." She paused again and shook her head. "But I digress. The second thing that happened is Derek lost his mother around this time last year. If that's not a reason to hate the holiday, I'm not sure what is."

Suddenly, Derek's disappearance over the last few days made sense: he was mourning the anniversary of his mother's death. And from what little she knew, he was doing it alone. No one should have to spend the holidays alone, especially someone suffering. "That is so sad," Grace replied, her thoughts turning to her own parents. The holidays had always been the hardest for her too, but she, at least, had been blessed enough to have Granny.

"I think you know what you need to do," Granny said to Grace.

Yes, she did know. It was time to bury the hatchet with Derek. Now all she had to do was figure out how.

Katherine gave Grace a sympathetic look. "Do we have any other plans for the day, dear?"

Grace gave Katherine an appreciative look in return. "We are supposed to go caroling with the drama club tonight! The kids are going to wear their costumes from the play!" Grace told them, grateful for the change in topic. "Once Grant has the total from the sales we made this morning, we'll know how much money we have to spend buying groceries at the store."

"You use the money from the pancake breakfast to buy groceries?" Katherine asked, her brow furrowed in confusion.

"Yes, for the people we sing carols to," Grace explained. "It was such a lovely experience last year, I just had to repeat it this year. Even though I tried to come up with new things for the guests to do," she hurried to add.

Carl reached over and patted her hand. "I wouldn't have minded if we did the exact same thing," he assured her.

"And I'm looking forward to the caroling tonight. I agree the experience last year was particularly moving. Plus, the kids will be a fun addition. I'm sure the people we will sing to will get a kick out of seeing them in costume!"

It was a relief to hear him say that. There were still a couple of hours until dinner, so she decided to propose a board game to pass the time. And while she was at it, she might just try to call Derek a time or two...hundred!

Christmas Eve!

G race stared out the sliding door as she snuggled a sleeping Piper in her arms. It was almost time to head back and round up her guests for the big Christmas Eve play, and she still hadn't managed to get ahold of Derek. Would he show up to give the introduction like he'd promised? Or would he ghost them a second time?

"I'm not sure I've ever seen you this stressed out before," Cole said as he came up behind her and wrapped his arms around her waist. "What's got you so wound up?"

"Too many things," she said, still staring at a random tree in the distance.

Cole rested his chin on the top of her head. "Want to tell me about them?"

Where should she even start? "I'm concerned about Derek, tonight is supposed to be the grand finale of my Traditional Christmas Experience, and this was supposed to be our wedding day," she let out in a whoosh.

He took a deep breath and let it out slowly. "That is quite the list," he agreed. "I love that you're able to show compassion to someone who hasn't been kind to you, but you can only do what you can do regarding Derek."

"Yes, but we've both lost parents, so we know what he's going through," Grace argued. "I just feel like I need to do something."

Cole turned her around to face him. "When I lost my mom, I went through a really dark time, so I get it," he said gently. "But how Derek chooses to handle his grief is up to him. If he doesn't want to let people in, you can't force him."

Grace's heart ached for both Cole and Derek. Sometimes life was so unfair. "You're right," she said reluctantly. "I just wish I hadn't antagonized him. Maybe then he'd answer my calls."

"Let's move on to your second concern," Cole prompted. "Why are you worried about the play?"

It was hard to switch gears, but she tried. "I really want tonight to be special. The kids worked so hard on this play, but I'm worried the guests will end up disappointed. It's not exactly Broadway-level, you know?"

One side of Cole's mouth lifted in a smile. "What matters is the message in the play, not the caliber of the actor delivering it. And most of your guests are parents—they'll see this through the eyes of love, not critique."

"I suppose you're right, again," she admitted. "I'm being a jerk worrying about this. I just can't seem to help it."

"That's because you're a bit of a perfectionist," Cole teased. "Remember last Valentine's Day when you lost it over the parking situation downtown?"

Grace groaned. "And you told me to stop taking responsibility for other people's problems?"

"I'm not sure those were my exact words, but yes," he chuckled. "This is Conor's area—let him shine."

He was right, as usual. The play was going to be amazing. To think otherwise was to doubt her friends, and she didn't want to do that.

"It's the last one that's really bothering you, isn't it?" he asked softly. When she looked up at him with tears in her eyes, he gently removed Piper from her arms and pulled her into his. "A piece of paper won't change how I feel about you, you know—it only makes it official. You're already my wife in my heart."

His beautiful words only made her cry harder. "I love you," she whispered against his neck.

"I love you, too, baby girl. I always will."

They held each other as long as they dared, then slowly pulled apart.

"We better go," he said quietly.

Grace nodded. "Will you stay with me tonight? I want to wake up next to you on our first Christmas morning."

"I'd like that, too," he grinned. "We can leave Max and Ruby here, but I'm not sure the little terror can be trusted," he added, nodding toward Piper, who was now innocently cleaning herself on the couch.

"We'll bring her with us," Grace replied, already calculating the logistics. Once Jackie had officially left, the twins had moved into Rebekah's room, allowing Grace to reclaim her bedroom. If she locked Piper in there, it should keep her out of trouble for the night.

"Sounds good," he said, grabbing his coat. "Are you ready?"

"As ready as I'll ever be!"

***

The trip to the high school had been uneventful. Molly and Grant had already had everyone loaded on the bus and ready to go when Grace and Cole arrived, so all they had to do was drop Piper off and join the others. Getting everyone inside the auditorium had been a different story. The place was packed with people, and since the tickets didn't include assigned seats, finding blocks of available chairs had proved difficult. When that was finally sorted, Grace left Cole, Granny, and Gladys to go backstage and find Conor.

"Looks like the kids' worst fear was for nothing," Grace said by way of greeting. "There's a packed house out there!"

Conor looked at Grace in a panic. "I know, and the kid who plays Scrooge just started puking because of it."

"Oh no," Grace said in concern. "Is he okay?"

"I'm sure it's just a bad case of stage fright, but Grace, what am I going to do? He can't perform in that condition, and there's no one to take his place!"

This was the kind of problem she'd been dreading not even an hour ago, and she hoped this wasn't some sort of self-fulfilling prophecy she was responsible for. "I thought all actors had an understudy or something like that?"

Conor stared at her for a moment. "This is a high school play, not a Broadway musical," he said in frustration. He took a breath and shook his head. "I'm sorry, that was rude. My point is that we didn't have enough kids for understudies, so I had to hope and pray everyone would stay healthy. Looks like that was a mistake."

"What was a mistake?" asked Derek as he walked up to them.

Grace eyed Derek as an idea formed in her mind. "I know, Derek could play the part of Scrooge! He'd be perfect!"

"Okay, seriously, what is it with you and this obsession you have with me being Scrooge? It's gotten really old, Grace," Derek said, his cheeks flushed with anger.

Conor stepped closer to Grace and put his hands up in a pleading manner. "The kid who's supposed to play Scrooge is sick, and we need a replacement. Please tell me you're willing to take his place?"

Derek looked between Conor and Grace, confusion replacing some of his anger. "Are you serious, or is this another one of her little games?" he asked, pointing to Grace.

It was hard not to take that personally, but Grace remembered what she'd learned about Derek the day before and managed to rein in her temper. "We're serious," she said earnestly. "Please say you'll help."

"Why can't Conor do it? I heard he's supposed to be the actor," Derek replied.

"Because I'm in charge of all the backstage stuff, and there's no one who could take my place," Conor explained. "Please," he begged.

Grace could see that Derek was considering it, but she had no idea how to give him that final nudge.

"I don't even know the lines," Derek said in exasperation.

Conor grabbed a script off a nearby desk and handed it to him. "You can study in between scenes, and Grace and I can make cue cards to hold up on the side of the stage." He turned to her. "You don't mind, do you?"

"Of course not," Grace said immediately. She'd been looking forward to watching the play, but when duty called, she answered.

"Fine," Derek said reluctantly. "What should I wear? I highly doubt some high school kid's costume will fit me."

"We'll do the best we can." Conor rushed off to find supplies, leaving Derek and Grace alone.

"I wanted to apologize," Grace said slowly. She wasn't sure how to approach him without putting him on the defensive. "I should not have antagonized you, and I'm sorry."

Derek raised his brows. "So, you're finally admitting that it was you who sent those cards?"

"No," Grace shook her head. "That still wasn't me. I'm admitting that I've acted childish and petty when it comes to you, and I'm embarrassed and ashamed of that."

He took a deep breath and let it out slowly. "While I appreciate that, I don't understand why you refuse to own up to the card incidents. They're not criminal offenses; they were just upsetting for what they were."

"Which is?" she asked, genuinely curious.

"Personal," he admitted reluctantly. "They felt deeply personal."

Grace could understand that, but what she couldn't understand was how he thought she was capable of that? They were practically strangers. It just wasn't possible for her to know him well enough to hit him so close to home. A fact she felt necessary to share with him. "Do really think a stranger is capable of getting that personal with you?"

The question appeared to catch him off guard, as he stumbled a bit over the lines he was reading out loud. "I don't know," he finally replied. He ran a hand through his hair, causing it to stick up at odd angles. "All I know is no one else has a motive."

"You keep repeating that as if it's an affirmation of guilt," Grace told him. "But all it means is that no one you can think of has a motive. Not that no one else could be responsible."

Since the conversation was going nowhere, Grace chose to focus on making cue cards instead. When a text message from Cole came through, she quickly apprised him of the situation, and then went back to work. Somehow she would find a way to get through the Derek, it would just have to wait until after the play.

Once the play started, there was no time to worry about anything other than positioning herself somewhere where Derek could see her, and the audience could not. Since he was required to move about the stage, Grace found herself running from side to side so much, she was about to collapse by the time the cast took their final bow. Somehow they had done it, they'd saved the play.

Derek, for his part, had been a pro. Unless you knew better, you would never have been able to tell he hadn't been cast in the part of Scrooge all along. As they gathered backstage after the play, everyone cheering and laughing, Derek stood off to the side.

"Is that a hint of a smile I see?" Grace teased.

He scowled at her, then laughed. "You caught me," he replied. "I hate to say it, but that was actually fun. I can't remember the last time I actually felt like I was a part of something."

Grace stilled at his words, too afraid to ruin the moment by saying something dumb. "You did a great job," she praised. "Everyone did. I was amazed at how well everyone performed out there."

"I was amazed, too. I hate to admit it, but my expectations were pretty low. In fact, I had planned to leave right after I gave the introduction."

"In my admittedly limited experience, everything happens for a reason," Grace replied absentmindedly. She'd been listening, but her attention had been caught by Cole who was waving to her from the hallway. "I need to go, but I really appreciate you stepping up," Grace told Derek. "And I know everyone else does to."

Derek nodded, but his attention had moved to his phone, and he appeared to only be half-listening.

"Hey," Grace said as she prepared to leave. "We would love it if you came by the house tomorrow. There will be a big turkey dinner, games, Christmas music, and probably everything else you hate," she teased.

He looked up in surprise. "You're inviting me to your house on Christmas?" he asked, both brows raised.

"Yes, I am, and I hope you accept my invitation. But if you don't, I wish you a very Merry Christmas."

Grace left before he could respond, hopeful he would take her words to heart. If he didn't, at least she'd tried, though she wished there was more she could do.

***

The ride back to the house was filled with laughter and chatter about the play. To Grace's relief, her guests had loved it. A few even said it was the best play they'd ever seen—praise she'd be sure to pass along to Conor and the kids.

When they arrived home, everyone but Cole and Granny retired to their rooms.

"I'd say this was another success," Granny said proudly. "Between the caroling last night and the play tonight, I think we've all been reminded of the true meaning of Christmas."

An image of Derek flashed through Grace's mind. She hoped Granny was right—and that this particular Scrooge was no exception.

Cole put an arm around Granny's shoulders and helped her to her room, then returned with a large box wrapped in gold paper.

"She said we should open this in private," Cole told Grace, leading the way upstairs.

"Do you know what it is?" Grace asked. She scooped up Piper as Cole opened the door. The cat meowed in protest, foiled in her attempt to escape. Grace laughed and set her gently on the bed next to the present.

"Only one way to find out," Cole said, pulling a small knife from his pocket. "Do you want to do the honors?"

Grace nodded and carefully cut the bow and paper. She had to move a curious Piper out of the way before lifting the lid—and gasped when she saw the beautiful, hand-stitched quilt inside.

Tears stung her eyes as Cole lifted it from the box and spread it out on the bed. "It's beautiful," she whispered, taking in every inch of the blue and white fabric.

"It's a wedding quilt," he said softly.

She looked up. "How do you know?" Blue and white were their wedding colors, but still...

"She told me a couple of months ago she was making one for us," he said. "She wanted us to have something to keep us warm on long, chilly nights."

Piper hopped into the box and rustled through the tissue paper.

Grace thought back to the stories Granny had told her—of loss and pain, but also hope and resilience. This quilt was more than a blanket. It was a gift of love, sewn by the hands of the woman who had spent her life loving her. No amount of gold, frankincense, or myrrh could compare.

Cole wrapped his arms around Grace and held her as they stared at the quilt. "I almost don't want to use it. I'm afraid it'll get ruined."

She leaned back against him and nodded. "I agree, but it would be a shame to hide it away. I don't think I could bear to pack it up."

"We'll just have to be careful, then."

They laughed as Piper jumped out of the box and curled up in the center of the quilt.

Grace turned in Cole's arms, wrapped hers around his neck, and pulled his face down to hers. "Merry Christmas, Cole," she whispered between kisses.

"Merry Christmas, my beautiful Grace."

Merry Christmas!

Grace opened her eyes and smiled as she stretched; it was officially Christmas! She turned to Cole, who was, of course, already awake and waiting for her with open arms. "Merry Christmas!" she said as she snuggled close to him.

"Merry Christmas!" he whispered back. "What do we do first?" he asked.

That was a good question. "Do we need to run out to the farm real quick and feed the animals?" she asked. She should have asked that last night, but had forgotten in all the excitement.

"No, Riley's going to do that before he comes here," Cole replied. He played with her hair with one hand while petting Piper with the other. The little furball had been quick to pounce on his chest the second she'd discovered he was awake.

Grace grinned as she watched the two of them. At this point, it seemed Piper might be more Cole's cat than hers, but she didn't mind. They were her little family, and that's all that mattered to her. "I guess that means I need to get up and start breakfast," Grace mused. Jilly had prepared some baked goods for the kids the day before, so all Grace needed to do was pop some breakfast casseroles in the oven, prepare coffee, and get it all set out on the breakfast bar when it was ready. Pretty easy for a holiday meal.

Her eyes grew wide as she remembered the turkey needed to go in the oven as well. "I better get down there," she said as she hopped out of bed.

"Just a minute," Cole replied as he got up and made his way to his overnight bag. He pulled a small box out of a side pocket and handed it to her. "I wanted to give you this before all the chaos starts," he chuckled.

She accepted the box and carefully opened the wrapping paper, unveiling a beautiful silver locket. She opened the clasp to discover a picture of the two of them on one side, and the inscription: I'll love you forever on the other side. Grace stared at the locket for a moment. "I love it!" She gasped as tears stung the corners of her eyes. "Will you help me put it on?" She asked as she handed him the necklace and lifted her hair out of the way.

Cole draped the necklace around her neck, then kissed her cheek. "This way, you'll always have a reminder of how much I love you," he whispered in her ear.

Grace held up her left hand. "This is the reminder I need," she replied as she pointed to her engagement ring. "But I will gladly accept a reminder I can keep close to my heart." She walked over to her dresser and pulled a box out of the top drawer and handed it to him. "You're not easy to shop for," she teased. "But I hope you like it."

He opened the box and pulled out a picture frame, his mouth opening in shock as he looked at the picture. "How did you do this?" he asked as he showed her the picture of him and his mother in front of the Christmas tree.

"I spent a lot of time compositing different photos together," she explained. "I remembered how much you said those decorations meant to your mom, so I thought maybe it would be nice to have a picture of the two of you with them..." Grace trailed off as she watched his facial expressions change. He wasn't always the easiest person to read, and right now she wasn't sure if she'd done something good, or bad. "If I've overstepped..."

Cole's head shot up and he quickly pulled her into his arms. "No, not at all. I just—this is truly the most thoughtful gift anyone has ever given me. Thank you," he said as he held her tight.

A sense of relief washed over her as she held him. She'd spent days trying to come up with the perfect gift, but nothing had ever seemed right. And then inspiration had hit and well, here they were.

"We better get downstairs," he said, finally releasing her.

Grace smiled up at him and nodded. She then took a second to cherish the moment, before taking his hand and leading the way downstairs.

***

It was almost time for Christmas dinner when Grace finally had a moment to catch her breath. She'd barely had breakfast out before her guests came down, and it was non-stop laughter and fun from then on. Friends had begun to arrive soon after, and before she'd known it, the house was bursting at the seams.

As she made her way to the kitchen to check on the turkey, the doorbell rang. Confused, she looked around, but everyone she knew was already there. Then it hit her—it was probably Rebekah's mom, back for another round of drama. Well, Grace was not about to let the woman ruin Christmas for her best friend.

With determined steps, she marched to the front door, threw it open, stepped out onto the porch, and then slammed the door behind her. Only, it wasn't Jackie waiting out in the cold—it was Derek.

"Oh," she said in surprise.

Derek's eyes widened at the unexpected greeting. "I take it you're not happy to see me," he joked.

"I'm so sorry," Grace said, her hand going to her mouth in horror. "I thought you were someone else, and, well... Merry Christmas?" she said lamely.

To her immense relief, Derek laughed. "I'm pretty sure I had that coming regardless."

"Please, come in," Grace said, opening the door and stepping back to give him room to pass.

"Um, actually, I just stopped by to tell you that I'm sorry," he said, his hand going to his neck. "I talked to Allen last night and he admitted he was the one who sent me those cards."

Grace gasped as she closed the door once more to keep the heat in. "Why would he do that?"

"It turns out he's been worried about me for a while now, and thought asking me to take over as mayor might help me get out of my funk." He ran a hand through his hair. "Honestly, I think he hoped you would inject some Christmas spirit into my cold, black heart, and those cards were meant to help guide me along the way or something."

"Just as the ghosts guided Scrooge," Grace said, nodding along as she realized the genius of Mayor Allen's plan. "That was very clever of him."

"I'm glad you get it," Derek said, sounding somewhat annoyed. "Because this is all still a little crazy to me. Anyway, you told me repeatedly you weren't the one sending the cards, and I refused to believe you. So, this is me saying I'm sorry for that."

Grace surprised them both by giving him a hug. "Apology accepted! Now, you're just in time for dinner, so why don't we go inside and get out of the cold? It's freezing out here!"

Derek hugged her back but shook his head. "I don't want to intrude, so I'm going to leave you to it."

"Nonsense," Grace said, grabbing his hand and pulling him along. "Winterwood has a rule that no one spends Christmas alone. And as the mayor, it is your duty to follow the rules!"

"I'm pretty sure you just made that up," he said with a laugh.

"Maybe, but do you really want to risk it?"

He motioned for her to go in front of him with his free hand. "Lead the way."

Once they were inside, Grace handed Derek off to Conor, Cassie, Evie, Jake, and Lyda, and left him to help Conor regale the group with tales of the backstage madness from the play the night before. She then went to the kitchen to help Katherine, Jilly, and Rebekah finish preparing dinner.

As she looked around at all the smiling faces, she felt her heart burst with love and joy. Especially when her eyes locked with a certain cowboy, who just so happened to be snuggling with a tiny furball while laughing at something Granny was saying.

There were still things that needed to be settled. Jilly and Bea still needed to finalize the sale of Bea's Bakery, and Jackie was still out there plotting. But for today, all that mattered was they were all together.

"Merry Christmas!" Grace shouted over the noise.

"Merry Christmas!" they all shouted back.

Afterword

Dear Reader,

Thank you so much for reading my book! I really hope you loved this one, there are scenes in here that are very close to my heart.

I had initially planned to squeeze Cole and Grace's wedding into this book, until a dear friend talked me out of it, so all of their talk about taking time and giving their wedding its proper due, was directed at me! So, Countdown to a Wedding will be coming soon.

Up next will be Countdown to New Beginnings. It will pick up the day after Christmas and will feature new guests, new drama, and the continuation of Rebekah's story. However, Grace will remain the main character.

Thank you so much for going on this journey with me!
Happy Reading! -Dianna